Please feel free to send me an email. Just know that my publisher filters these emails. Good news is always welcome.

Cheryl F. M. - cheryl_fm@awesomeauthors.org

Sign up for my blog for updates and freebies!
cheryl-fm.awesomeauthors.org

I0670910

About the Publisher

BLVNP Incorporated, A Nevada Corporation, 340 S. Lemon #6200, Walnut CA 91789, info@blvnp.com / legal@blvnp.com

DISCLAIMER

Praise for Bad For Me

I grew to love the book even more as seconds went by. My eyes were glued to it for an entire day because I just couldn't put it down. It was so beautiful. The characters were enchanting just like the writing itself.
-Bewitching Angel, Goodreads

I personally love this book and it's so easy to fall in love with the main characters and their personalities. I totally recommend this book to anyone who wants to read a good romantic novel, with hardships of life but still end up together.
-Elizabeth, Goodreads

I absolutely love this book! It is such an amazing romance novel that makes me swoon every time I read it! I'm so excited that this is out there for more then just us wattpad readers!
-Casey Wettach, Goodreads

Absolutely love this book! I read Bad For Me several times a week. It's one of the best books I have ever read and recommend it to anyone who loves romance and humor stories!
-Karina Young, Goodreads

One of my first loves.. A love story with gentle curves.. Tragic, emotional, funny and witty.. Can make you laugh, cry, jump and dance all at the same time.... Characters are easy to fall in love with..
A must read book..
-Miraz Deka, Goodreads

Bad For Me

By: Cheryl F. M.

BLVNP

ISBN: 978-1-68030-822-8

Table of Contents

To my sister, who has motivated and encouraged me to continuing writing even when I felt like giving up. Love you dear!

FREE DOWNLOAD

Get these freebies and MORE when you sign up for the author's mailing list!

cheryl-fm.awesomeauthors.org

CHAPTER 1-THE
BEGINNING

Olivia

I glared at my oldest brother Nate and crossed my arms. "Nate, please get out of my room now."

Nate just stared at me with a smirk on his face as he leaned against the doorframe. "I will, but only after you hear me out."

I scowled and had to hold back the overwhelming urge to throw something at him. "Fine. What do you want to talk about? I have a flight tomorrow morning, and I need to pack."

Nate raised an eyebrow and grinned. "I know, and I'm telling you, you better not have any funny ideas while you're in London. No hooking up, no drugs, and no booze."

I frowned and narrowed my eyes. Who does my oldest brother think he is? And surely, he knows me well enough that I would never do drugs. I felt the urge to throw a pillow at him… or maybe a purse.

"Nate, seriously, I'm an adult. Treat me as such. Also, please get out of my room." I repeated impatiently and watched as my oldest brother roll his eyes at me. At that moment, I felt like I was a kid again.

Nate made a face and shrugged casually, still leaning against the doorframe of my room. "I'm not leaving until you agree to my rules." He gave me a bright mocking grin as he sang his words out. His eyes were glinting with amusement.

I sighed exasperatedly and crossed my arms. "Okay, yes. Get out." I pointed the door, and Nate gave me a smirk before his face softened as he watched me pack my stuff into the little black suitcase on my bed.

"I don't even see why you're working as an air stewardess of all things. You can work at the family company or something."

This topic was an ongoing conversation for the past two years of my life. You can say that my family was very wealthy, and I am an heiress. However, I don't want to depend on my family's wealth for a living nor do I want to work in the family business. I want a job of my own. I feel that being an air stewardess allowed me to earn my own income and travel a little. It is one of my dreams to travel around the world.

As I packed my small black suitcase, my second older sister, Elena, entered my room and knocked. Giving her a distracted smile as she sat on my bed, I asked, "Hey Ellie, do you need anything?"

She shook her head, and her dark hair bounced as she smiled. "No, I just wanted to ask you if you remembered what's going on this Thursday?"

I frowned and slowly shook my head as I tried to remember any events that would be taking place on the said date. "Nope. Sorry, nothing rings a bell."

Ellie grinned before prompting, "My engagement party will be this Thursday!"

My eyes widened. "Oh god, I completely forgot about it. Ellie, I'm sorry." I apologized and bit my lip as I turned to face her.

"It's alright, but you will be there, right? You're my sister, and I want you to be there." Ellie hugged me and grinned.

I nodded. "Definitely. I'll be there, and I'll be back on Wednesday." I reassured her before stopping as I realized something. "Wait a minute, why are you so chirpy about it?" I questioned. I had a hunch that Ellie was up to something. She was never good at hiding or keeping things a secret.

Ellie bit her lip and averted her eyes. "Uh. Nothing. It's just that Scott has a younger brother who is only one year older than you and—"

"No, absolutely not. I'm not interested in blind dates. Not with the guys you and Lily are trying to set me up with, not even Scott's younger brother," I said and narrowed my eyes at Ellie. At least she had the decency to be embarrassed. I saw her expressions change from embarrassment to disbelief and finally, annoyance.

"Am I that obvious?" She sat on my bed, and I did the same.

"Yes. It's pretty clear. At least try to be less obvious about it like Lily. I don't see why you and Lily have to keep setting me up."

Ellie crossed her arms defensively as she sniffed, obviously miffed that I had seen through her act. "It gets lonely if you're single. All Lily, mum, and I want is to see you happy," she said.

"I know, it's just that I'm happy as I am now."

She hugged me. "Okay. As long as you're happy, but Scott's younger brother is really, really hot."

I rolled my eyes and zipped my suitcase. "I'm not interested, Ellie."

I could sense that Ellie was pouting but sighed as she responded, "Alright. Anyway, Mom called to tell me to ask you to come down for dinner."

I nodded and pushed my blonde hair back. "Okay. I'll be down in a second. I just have to pack some last few items. You can go first."

Ellie stood up from my bed. "Okay. Be quick." With that, she walked out of my room.

As I headed down for dinner, I could hear my brothers yelling in the living room. I rolled my eyes. Even though I was the youngest in the family of six children, my brothers never seemed to grow up.

"Whoop! Score! Ha! Take that, you bloody losers!"

"What the fuck, Nate? I'm so going to get you for this!"

"Jake, go get Tristan!"

I ignored them and walked to the dining room, where my oldest sister Lily was with her husband, Parker, and their two children, Phillip, and Penny. Ellie was there already, sitting next to mom and dad. I took the vacant chair beside my father.

"Just to double check, everyone in this family will be home for Ellie and Scott's engagement party, right?" my mom questioned as she glanced at all of us for confirmation.

Lily and Parker said yes while I simply gave a nod. On the other hand, all three of my brothers yelled, "Hell yes."

"Language!"

I snickered at my mom's narrowed gaze towards my brothers.

"Of course, we have to. We'll be here to see if Scott has any second thoughts and stuff." I tried not to laugh at Ellie's horrified expression at Nathaniel's announcement.

"Mom, you've got to do something. Please!" She begged while shooting evil stares at our brothers.

"You boys are going to interrogate Scott on Thursday?" my dad asked with his eyebrows raised.

"Yeah. All three of us." Nathaniel grinned. Tristan cleared his throat, and Nathaniel sighed before grumbling, "Two of us."

My dad wrapped an arm around my mom's waist and said cheerily, "Well, I'll join you."

Ellie shook her head, and her shoulders slumped in defeat. "I thought that you approved of Scott!"

My dad grinned. "Yeah, I did, but he may jilt you at the altar. And no daughter of mine will go through that." At this statement, I was thankful that I didn't have a boyfriend. Lily started laughing while I tried not to laugh at Ellie's horrified face.

"Dad!" Ellie glared at dad while my brothers smirked smugly at her.

"So Liv, you don't have a boyfriend yet, right?" I glanced up at Jake, Nathaniel's twin, and sipped some soup.

"No. I'm not interested in having one."

"Good, you're still twenty-three. No rush." My dad butted in as he ate.

"Great. There goes my chance of getting eloped," I replied dryly.

I watched in satisfaction as Nathaniel tensed. "You're getting eloped?"

I shook my head in frustration. "No! It's called sarcasm. God, you're stupid."

Jake glared at me mockingly. "Not funny, Liv."

Rolling my eyes at them, I started to eat and hoped that dinner would pass soon.

Lily was the oldest in the family while Nathaniel and Jacob — also known as Jake — were twins. They were followed soon after by my sister Ellie, and finally, another twin: Tristan and me.

Being the youngest wasn't a walk in the park, especially in this family.

Drake

"Okay, Drake, I have something really important to say, and I need you to listen to me." I glanced up curiously at my older brother Scott and slid my phone into my pocket.

"Okay, you're scaring me. What is it?" I grinned as my older brother rolled his eyes at me.

"I'm engaged."

"And?" I raised an eyebrow and commented dryly.

Scott frowned. "Yeah, that's it. I'm engaged. Why aren't you freaking out?"

I smirked in response. My brother thought that he was being sneaky with his girlfriend who I have yet to meet. But, honestly, was I born yesterday?

"I knew you had a secret girlfriend all along, and well, to hear that you're engaged is not that big of a deal. I mean, sure, I'm annoyed that you didn't tell me or let me meet her, but it's your choice."

Scott grimaced, most probably sulking, that he wasn't that good at keeping secrets before smiling at me. "Alright, whatever. Yes, I have a girlfriend who is now my fiancée. I'm sorry for not telling you. You're bound to mess it up somehow."

I shot him a scowl. It was nice to know that my own brother had such little faith in me. "Thanks for your everlasting confidence in me, brother."

"It's true, and you know it. Anyway, her name is Elena Ford, and we've been together for three years." Scott grinned before shoving a playful punch in my arm.

I blinked and shrugged before replying, "Okay. When can I meet her?"

Scott beamed, happy that I was taking his *not-so-secret* news easily without making a fuss.

"This Thursday, her parents would be throwing an engagement party for us at their family home. You can go, right? Seeing that the only family member I have is you. Mom is in Hawaii, and Dad is in Scotland."

"Yeah, yeah, sure. What's the dress code?"

Scott shrugged. "Really fancy. Wear a suit with a bow tie."

"That fancy with so much fuss? Why not elope? Surely, that is easier."

"I don't have a death wish! She has three brothers that all play football. The eldest used to be in the army. So, you can imagine their size." Scott gave me a pointed look, and I snorted, already imagining the three tall, muscular guys pounding my older brother for eloping with their sister.

"Three brothers? That's a lot. Does she have any other siblings? Also, you're only twenty-seven. You don't have to get married this early, you know."

Scott sighed before frowning at me. "Look, I love her, and nothing you say or do can change that. Yes, Ellie has two sisters, an older one and a younger one."

"You're hopeless, but it's your death wish." I shook my head and shrugged. It doesn't mean that because I didn't share my brother's idea of commitment, I was going to discourage him from it.

Scott narrowed his eyes at me before exhaling heavily. "Whatever, man. It's my life, not yours. Also, do remember to wear a bow tie. Aren't you going to pack your bags? You're leaving tomorrow morning, aren't you?"

"Yeah, I already did. The groupies in London are worth a second look, you know?"

Feeling a disapproving stare at me, I looked up to see Scott looking at me with exasperation. "One day, some girl is gonna knock your world off its axis, and you're gonna see that being a man-whore is not that appealing."

I shook my head and smirked. "Sure. She can try, but I like the way my life is now."

Scott simply shook his head as head and went back to his room.

CHAPTER 2-THE FLIGHT

Drake

I could say that first class seating was pretty great.

"So, Rick, how is Lena? Still cursing you for getting her pregnant after two kids?" I smirked at Rick, my manager, a happily married man of five years who is saddled with a wife and two kids with another one on the way.

"No, she's much quieter now that she's easily tired which is a bad or good thing depending on how you look at it."

I laughed. "This is why I'm not waiting in line to get hitched."

"You just don't know what you're missing out on." Rick grinned.

I grimaced and made a face, hinting that I completely doubt him. "I don't see how an annoying wife and a non-stop crapping baby would make you feel like you're the champion of your world."

Rick laughed. "As I said, it depends on how you see it. Okay, shut up now. I have to write out the terms and agreements on your new contract and run through some parts of it with you, not to mention, the rest of your publicity campaign."

I snorted and turned away from him. I eyed a redhead, and when she noticed me staring, I gave her a small wink. The redhead blushed and turned away. This was too easy.

As the plane was about to take off, the air stewards started to come by and checked up on us. My eyes caught onto one particular air stewardess. She had blonde hair, groomed cleanly in some hairstyle, which further emphasized her pretty green eyes and good facial features. And all I could do was stare.

"Henderson! You have that look again." My head snapped towards Rick as he smirked at me.

"What look?" I turned back to where the blonde air stewardess was and almost groaned out loud as she bent down, her skirt tightening around her round ass.

"That look when you want to go on a sex rampage."

"What? What the hell are you talking about?" I scoffed, earning a snide look from him before giving his full attention back to my contract.

"She's pretty, but not my type. Lena is my type."

I snorted and glanced back at the blonde stewardess who was nearing me. *God, she is gorgeous as hell.*

"Excuse me." I grinned as she came towards me. *God, she is even more gorgeous up close.*

Beside me, Rick was nudging me incessantly. "Drake, what the hell do you think you're doing?" He was practically shouting in my ear. *Sheesh, he needs a life.* I rolled my eyes. He was such a killjoy.

"Yes, how can I help you?" she asked politely with a smile.

I smirked. "Do you think the bathrooms here can fit two people? Like you and me?" I asked smoothly with a suggestive grin.

Meanwhile, Rick sighed and slapped his forehead the minute those words came out of my mouth. I knew she got the hint and was going to agree. *Who would resist me?* I was Drake Henderson, famous racer and also known for womanizing.

The blonde stewardess stared blankly at me, unimpressed, before she narrowed her eyes and the smile on her face tightened. She was still composed and polite despite her eyes showing how much she would love to kill me.

"I apologize, sir. If there is nothing else, I will take my leave." With a sharp curt nod of her head, she raised herself to her full height and left.

I could feel Rick staring at me. I tore my eyes away from the stewardess and looked at Rick's shocked face. After a few beats, he started laughing. *What the fuck just happened?* I glanced back at the blonde air stewardess one last time as she walked away.

"Oh, wow. She rejected you. This is the first time I have ever seen this happen! Wait till your crew knows about this. Drake Henderson gets rejected for the very first time!" Rick burst into laughter. He was amused as hell while I was stunned beyond belief. I could not believe what just happened. I gritted my teeth. I had never been so mad.

Gathering my wits, I narrowed my eyes. As I turned to Rick, I glared. "Shut the fuck up! No one hears about this!"

Rick smirked at me and waved his phone in front of my face. "I just told everyone."

I slumped back into my seat. "What the fuck just happened? Who the hell does she think she is?"

Rick snorted. "You sound way too egoistic now. Maybe all that car exhaust has gotten into your head and caused some brain damage."

"Just shut the hell up, Rick."

When we finally landed in London, I kept a lookout for the blonde air stewardess. Not that I was interested or anything, but during the entire flight, I had kept my eyes out for her. What I noticed was, when attending to other passengers, she would give them a polite smile. However, when she caught me looking at her, she gave me the evil eye.

What bloody fantastic luck.

"Come on, Drake. Stop eyeing the blonde. We got a meeting to go to," Rick called up to me before turning and leaving, obviously telling me to follow. I ignored him when I finally spotted her. About to head towards her and demand an explanation, I stopped when a man who was probably the same height as me went towards the blonde and hugged her tightly.

Clenching my jaw, I exhaled heavily and turned away. By now, Rick had finally realized that I wasn't behind him like he wanted and pulled me away. "Snap out of it, Drake. We got a meeting. It's your first rejection. Just take it lightly." I clenched my jaw sullenly and remained silent, turning back once more, hoping to catch one last glance at her, but she was already gone.

Olivia

I fumed as I ground my teeth. The nerve of that man! Who on earth did he think he was? His question was plain rude. Although he was very, very good-looking, I do not have sex with random strangers, especially in public!

It was a shame that he was really good-looking but had a personality that was just plain awful. I drummed my fingers in irritation against my bag. The mere thought of him was bringing back all the anger I had experienced earlier.

The man had gorgeous blue eyes, a nice set of lips, and a strongly defined jaw that had stubble on it. It also wasn't fair that he had a very attractive voice, and even his smirk was sexy as hell. Life wasn't fair at times. It simply wasn't. The man even had the bad boy image going on due to his black leather jacket and ruffled black hair where some of his fringes fell over his forehead.

He was such an egotistic arse. While he had been speaking, I had the urge to punch him in the face.

As I walked out of the airport, a grin came over my face as I spotted my twin, Tristan. He was probably my favorite brother as he never annoys me and is a really good listener. He used to play football until he became more interested in music. So, right now, Tristan has a really promising future in the music industry, and I couldn't be prouder of him.

The minute I exited the arrival hall, I rushed towards him and hugged him tightly. "What are you doing here? You didn't say you were coming!"

He flashed me a grin and shrugged. "Surprise, I thought I could pop by and visit the penthouse here for these two days."

I beamed and punched him playfully. "You should've told me."

Tristan grinned playfully. "Sorry, Liv. Anyway, let's be on our way to our London penthouse. That sounded really cool, didn't it?"

I grinned and rolled my eyes. "You're such a dork."

Tristan grinned and wriggled his eyebrows. "Yeah, baby sis, but I'm your favorite brother."

I snorted, not denying his claim. "So, how are things at home with all the planning of Ellie's party?"

Tristan shrugged. "As usual, Grandmother Leslie helped, so you know what that means."

I sighed. "Extravagant and over the top. Great, just great. So, who's on the invitation list?"

Tristan said flatly, "Everyone and anyone that she knows, Scott and his younger brother, and that's about it."

I mumbled in defeat, "Great. Just great. That's almost the entire population of New York."

Tristan laughed. "Let's stop talking and go to our London penthouse. Mom says there's a pool." He wiggled his eyebrows at me playfully, and I laughed as we headed to the exit of the airport.

We headed into the waiting black car with my brother. I handed my small luggage to Tristan, who helped put it into the boot while I got in the car. On the way to the penthouse, somehow, I couldn't stop thinking about that hot leather-jacket-wearing man even though he was an arse.

CHAPTER 3-THE COINCIDENTAL MEETING

Drake

"Drake! Do remember that the event is a black-tie event. Please, *please* dress appropriately."

I sighed heavily and rolled my eyes before watching my brother adjust his bow tie and his gelled hair.

"Who exactly are your future parents-in-law? Black-tie?"

Scott answered dryly, "You'll know later. Why do you look so annoyed? You've had that same annoyed expression on your face since you got back from London."

I scowled and turned away from him. That blonde air stewardess had been on my mind twenty-four-seven, and why not? She was the first woman ever to reject me. Who the heck would even reject me? No one! Well, only her, apparently. God, why the fuck was I even thinking about her now? I was never going to see her again, would I?

"Just drop the topic, Scotty. So, can I please wear a tie?"

My brother glanced at me before straightening his stance. "No, you can't, Drake. You need to wear a bow tie." He tossed me one, and I frowned in disgust before giving in. Even though I thought that bow ties were ridiculous, I wasn't going to make a fuss when Scott was obviously freaking out. His movements were harried, and he kept going back to the mirror to check his appearance.

Scott left the room, and I began tying the bow around my neck. Checking that my appearance was impeccable, I finally shrugged on the black suit jacket and messed about with my hair.

"Drake, hurry!" Scott shouted up the stairs, and I shifted my jaw before taking my time to walk down the stairs. Scott really sounded like a mom now. Sighing heavily, I left the room and began trudging down the stairs feeling like a pansy for wearing a bow tie.

"Fuck. Who the hell is your fiancée?"

Scott grinned at my astounded and amazed gaze at the huge white mansion. Scott smiled lovingly as he answered, "Ellie."

I rolled my eyes and punched his arm. "I know that."

Scott was about to reply when a woman walked out with a distinguished senior man following her. "Scott!"

I glanced at her with interest. Meanwhile, my brother had a silly grin on his face as he embraced the said woman and kissed her. "Hey, Ellie, we're not late, are we?"

I studied her, and all I could say was that she was pretty, but not my type. I preferred blondes, and my brother's fiancée had dark brown hair, bright green eyes which were filled with love as she hugged my brother back.

She was shorter than me by a few inches, and I could say for certain that I've never met her before. But somehow, she looked slightly familiar. I just couldn't place it. There was something quite familiar about her.

Ellie shook her head, smiling happily. "Nope, you're early because Dad made the chauffeur get you earlier since he wanted to talk to you. I tried to persuade him not to, but, you know, Nate backed Dad up."

Scott's face visibly changed with the news, and I tried not to laugh at how pale he got. "Yeah, anyway, Ellie, meet my younger brother, Drake. Drake, meet my fiancée, Elena, otherwise known as Ellie."

I grinned as she held out a hand for a shake. Instead, I took her hand and placed a kiss on it. "It's a pleasure to meet you, Miss Ford."

Ellie laughed and hugged me. "Welcome to the family!" She pulled away and turned to the senior man. "Edward, tell mom and dad that Scott and his brother have arrived. Don't worry. I'll be showing them to the lounge."

"Of course, Miss Ford."

Ellie turned to us and gave us a grin. "Come on, Scott. Hurry! You don't want to make my brothers wait now, do you?"

My brother let out a nervous laugh and shook his head. "No. Of course, not." My brother had been worrying about how to deal with Ellie's brothers ever since he told me on Monday.

Ellie laughed once more and brought us into the house. Again, I was stupefied; the interior of the house was grand and classy. Ellie led us through a hallway and into a room which I guessed was the lounge.

"Mom, Scott's here with his younger brother."

I glanced around interestedly, and my eyes landed on the oldest couple in the room before nodding my head in respect. Beside them were three men who are probably around my height or slightly shorter, but all of them were well-built and good-looking. Two of them were identical, and the last man looked familiar. The urge to find out was bothering me a lot.

On their left was a woman who had a baby and a little boy on her lap.

"Scott! How are you? You must be Drake. You look exactly the same as Scott. You're a racer, aren't you? Oh! Forgive me. I'm Ariana Ford. Please have a seat."

I offered a smile in response, "Hello, Mrs. Ford, and yes, I am. Do you enjoy the sport?"

Ariana shook her head. "Call me Ariana and no, but my husband does." I nodded in acknowledgment as I could feel all the males in the room scrutinize me. Goddamn, this is what it felt like for Scott all the time. But I guess for my brother, it was way worse. After all, he's marrying one of their own.

"Hi, I'm Lily. It's nice to meet you." The woman with the kids spoke up and smiled at me.

"It's nice to meet you too." I offered a polite smile.

Beside me, Scott was sitting nervously with Ellie holding his hand calmly.

"I'm Nathaniel." One of the twins said while assessing me.

"Jacob." A person who looked exactly like Nathaniel narrowed his eyes at me. "I'm Jacob's twin." *Well, that explains it. God, this was getting slightly annoying.* The smile on my face tightened, and I shoved one of my hands into the pockets of my jacket.

"I'm Tristan," said the annoyingly familiar man who I swear I've never met before. I resisted the urge to stare at him while I racked my brains on where I've seen him before.

"Oh! Has anyone seen Olivia?" Ariana spoke up and glanced around the room. Scott seemed to be relieved at the change of subject when a voice spoke up.

"I'm here! Sorry, I'm late. I had a wardrobe malfunction."

A mass of blonde hair sped past me as she went to sit next to Lily.

"You always have a wardrobe malfunction every day, Liv," Nate muttered.

The entire time, Olivia had her head bowed down as she meddled with her shoes. "Just shut up, Nate! I don't need your opinion."

Olivia snapped at Nate, and I shifted my jaw from the awkward silence that settled around the room.

Ariana cleared her throat, and Ellie perked up. "Oh, Olivia! Meet Drake, Scott's younger brother." Olivia looked up, and my jaw dropped as hers did.

"You!" Both of us yelled at the same time.

Olivia

I glared at the man in front of me. *It had to be him! Did that mean that he's...? Oh, god! This ass who asked me to have sex with him in a bathroom was going to be sort of related to me? Oh god. I'm so doomed. Although I had to admit, he still looked ruggedly hot even though he was clad in a suit. I was in trouble. What the heck was I going to do?*

"Wait, you two know each other?" a very confused Ellie asked as she glanced at us

God, even his name was attractive. I shook my head vigorously and gave her a loud 'No' while the ass said 'Yes.' I crossed my arms and stared at him condescendingly.

"No, I don't. What are you talking about?" I turned my head slightly and met my brothers questioning and suspicious glances. *Great, I'm going to be in so much trouble.*

"Anyway, Ellie, your grandparents would be here shortly from their vacation in Spain." My mom added to make the silence between Ellie, Lily, Dad, and Drake less awkward. I glanced under my lashes at Drake to see him staring intensely at me.

A devilish smirk curved on his mouth when he caught me staring back at him. Mortified at being caught, I hurriedly averted my eyes and turned away. Meanwhile, my brothers were talking to Scott about football and stuff while Ellie leaned on him lovingly and contributed to the conversation.

"Guests are arriving, Mrs. Ford." My mom turned to Edward, our butler. My mum gave Ellie and Scott a warm smile as she dismissed Edward. "Everyone, let's head to the party. Olivia, hon, I'd like to speak to you for a moment."

I sighed in defeat. My mother was fantastic at reading people.

Once the room cleared, my mother didn't waste any time before heading straight for the kill. "So, is there anything you want to tell me?" my mother asked as she sat beside me with a tender smile on her face. I bit my lip and blurted out everything to her. Somehow, my mom can always make me spill my darkest secrets to her with just one look.

Once I finished, she started to laugh. "Oh, Liv, he sounds exactly like your dad."

My expression remained stoic as my mother sighed and shook her head. "Alright, I trust that you would be a gracious host. Now, let's head to the party or Ellie will not be pleased. We wouldn't want that now, would we?"

I frowned, a crossed Ellie was a force not to be reckoned with. *Boy,* Scott was going to be in big trouble if he knew what Ellie was like when she became angry. It took someone that was extremely patient and well-versed in the skill of being charming to face her wrath.

On that thought, it would be extremely amusing to see Drake face Ellie's anger. A bright grin crossed my face at that image.

CHAPTER 4-THE ENGAGEMENT PARTY

Olivia

Sipping my glass of champagne while watching my sister and her fiancé dance, I couldn't help but notice that Ellie looked extremely happy. She was smiling giddily at her fiancé as he twirled her around. Scott had a warm smile on his face as he looked down at her lovingly, and I bit my lip at that.

I sighed in exasperation to see my brothers exchanging looks with each other while giving the occasional glance in Scott's direction and whispering conspiratorially.

"They are at it again, aren't they?" I looked beside me to see my eldest sister, Lily, sidling next to me with a glass of champagne in her hand.

I laughed and nodded my head. "Yeah. This time, it looks as if Jake is the ringleader."

"Yeah. The things they did to Parker. Well, with Nathaniel planning everything. Though I'm guessing, you got it lucky. I doubt Tristan would do anything to earn your annoyance and anger."

"Yes, I am extremely lucky. Tristan knows better. He's my twin after all."

Lily cracked a grin as she reminisced about the day that Nathaniel pranked Parker, her husband, the night before they got married.

Soon enough, the dreamy expression on my sister's face faded before she started to smile at me. "Loverboy is staring at you again."

I frowned and turned around to spot Drake staring at me with his smoldering blue eyes. I felt a blush creep onto my cheeks as I turned back to Lily's knowing smile.

"No, Lily. Really, no. We just had a nasty bump at the airport in London. That's all."

Lily smiled with a glint in her eyes. "Right. Anyway, Parker and I will be dancing now. Have fun with airport boy."

I frowned at Lily's words, and my scowl deepened when I felt him behind me. His presence was just too hard to ignore. After a moment, I turned around and there he was, facing me with a smirk on his handsome features. Once again, I resisted the urge to smack him.

"Care to dance?"

I narrowed my eyes before offering a tight, strained smile. "I'll have to apologize. I'm not interested." I turned away from him and sipped at my champagne flute, my eyes scanning the crowd in the room.

I could feel him smirking at me again, and I took my champagne flute before downing the entire thing. I needed more if I had to deal with this.

"Come on, give me a chance. Sorry about the incident in London. I didn't get to show you my charm. So, let's start over. Would you want to dance?"

"I'm not interested in dancing—" I was cut off when he held out his hand as an invitation to dance. I looked at him, trying not to show any expression on my face, but I'm pretty sure I failed. I could sense that my expression had softened. It must be a moment of weakness or the sexiness of his voice because I agreed.

"Fine, I'll dance with you. Just once, but do you even know how to dance? After all, you only drive around in circles for a living." I sarcastically added with a saccharinely sweet smile, hoping that he would get offended. I was so not over the entire airplane debacle.

Drake raised his eyebrows, and a smirk crossed his face as he led me to the dance floor. I cursed myself for letting my heartbeat speed up.

"For your information, darling, I do know how to dance, and my career choice is exhilarating. You should try it sometime." I placed my hand on his shoulder while he held my waist. And I have to admit, his hand on my waist felt kinda nice.

"Maybe, maybe not. I don't have a death wish."

He chuckled and twirled me around. "Like I said, it's exhilarating. And may I mention, you look beautiful? It certainly is a change from your uniform, though I liked your navy blue skirt better. It shows your long legs."

Immediately, all thoughts of how nice he seemed and how good he looked faded. His attitude was still terribly awful. I glowered at him before hissing at him quietly. "You're a pervert, a sex-crazed pervert." My hands were gripping onto his shoulders tightly as if preventing them from hitting him. I was yearning to right now. He was a total prat!

His face came closer to mine. "Like you aren't? You've been checking me out ever since you saw me."

I glared at him, furious that he knew I had been checking him out. In response and without thinking, I stomped hard on his right foot and stalked off. I heard him growl out in pain. It really must hurt considering I was wearing five-inch stilettos.

I heard guffawing, and I turned around to see my brothers roaring with laughter… at me… for stomping on Drake's foot. I glared at them and muttered, "Oh, grow up and stop being jerks."

At this moment, my mother walked up to me with a disapproving look on her face, and I sighed. Here comes the lecture.

✳✳✳✳✳✳✳✳✳✳✳✳✳

Drake

Fucking hell! That little vixen just stomped on my bloody foot! Anger and irritation were swimming in my veins, and I would love to throttle her pretty neck.

"I'm really sorry. I have absolutely no idea what Olivia was thinking. She was always the most stubborn and impulsive out of all of us."

"It's alright. It's my fault. I provoked her." I gritted my teeth as the ice pack numbed the pain on my foot while I thought of all the possible ways I could strangle her.

Lily, who I learned was the eldest of the Ford children, bit her lip and shook her head as her husband prodded at my foot.

"Still, she shouldn't have done that, and again, I apologize for her terrible behavior. Parker, is his foot alright?"

The last sentence was directed at her husband who I also learned was a doctor. "Yeah, his foot is fine, just some bruising due to the sharp point of the heel. Just ice it and stop provoking Olivia. She's dangerous when it comes to footwear."

Lily lightly smacked the back of Parker's head. "Hey, that's my sister you're talking about. He's right, though. Olivia once threw a slipper at Nathaniel, and it resulted into a bleeding nose. Alright, we should head for dinner now. Parker, where's Phillip and Penny?"

"Our children are with your Grandmother Leslie," Parker replied while still prodding my foot. "She was showing them off to some people she knew."

"Alright, let us go before our kids get too coddled. Drake, are you coming? You can walk, right?"

I tested my weight on my foot and nodded my head. "Yeah. It's not a problem. I'll be fine."

"Good. Let's go. You have yet to meet the rest. After all, we're going to be family. So, good luck with that." Lily smiled at me while leading me to the dining room.

At least half of the guests had already been seated, and Ellie headed towards me grinning. "Drake, there you are! I've been looking for you. I hope your leg is better. Anyway, you're sitting with Olivia. Good luck."

Great. My frown deepened. I headed towards Olivia and promptly sat down. She tensed for a short moment but quickly composed herself and threw a smug little smirk at me.

Her blonde locks swung over her shoulder as she asked sweetly, "Don't you have someone to bother? Oh right, you can't walk." She was obviously pleased in the state that I was while I glowered.

"No, I think I'll rather stay here to talk to my favorite blonde."

Olivia narrowed her eyes at me as she pressed her lips together into a thin line. She was pretty cute with her annoyed expression. Her eyes were squinted, lips pursed, and her brows furrowed.

"Funny. You're such an ass."

"But I bet that's what you like about me." She rolled her eyes and quietly snorted to not draw attention to us.

"Apparently, the pain has you talking nonsense," she answered sweetly before turning away.

"Feisty," I murmured under my breath, and she stepped on my foot again, the same fucking one she had stepped on earlier.

"Goddamnit!" I hissed, and my knee banged against the underside of the table.

I glared at her angrily as she smirked satisfactorily. "Stop being a big baby. It's just a little bruise."

"What the hell is your problem?"

"You're the problem."

"No, you're the problem. Not the other way round. You stepped, no, stomped on my foot twice."

"Well, if you had been nicer and not a jerk, tonight would have turned out differently."

"Different? How? You under me on a bed?" I smirked as her face turned a slight shade of pink as she crossed her arms over her chest, drawing my attention towards it.

"Hey, eyes up here! And, no. I meant that we would be more civilized, and I would not be stepping on your foot. Twice!"

My eyes drifted up to her annoyed face. She really was breathtaking. All the Fords were.

She scowled at me. "Anyway, leave me alone and do stop bothering me." With an elegant huff, she turned away.

I chuckled under my breath and glanced at Scott who was looking slightly dazed as an older woman chatted to him nonstop while Ellie was nodding and conversing back. I felt a tap on my shoulder and turned around to see the matriarch of the family smiling at me.

"Drake, would you like to stay at our house until the wedding? I have already proposed the idea to Scott, and he agreed. Ellie came up with the idea as this would make it easier to plan the wedding and its tiny details. Now, all that's left is you agreeing to it."

I glanced at Olivia to see her body posture tense with her eyes on her plate, pretending not to hear us. Smirking to myself, I smiled sincerely before answering, "If it is alright with you, it sounds fine. As long as you don't think we're imposing on you."

Ariana beamed. "You're not. You're going to be family. I'll let the housekeeping staff know. You can stay tonight and get your things tomorrow. Again, on behalf of Olivia, I'm apologizing for her inexcusable behavior."

I nodded and shrugged. "It's fine. It's my fault. Thank you for your hospitality."

Ariana grinned and shot a warning look at Olivia, who was still facing front.

Seeing that she was ignoring me, I whispered to her, "Looks like I can't stay away now, can I?"

"Oh, shut up."

A moment of silence had passed before a voice spoke up, "Olivia, dear, where have you been hiding? I've been looking for you."

Beside me, Olivia groaned silently as she turned around. A warm smiled slipped onto her face as she responded, "Hi, Grandmother Leslie. I wasn't hiding. I was just, uh, preoccupied with something."

The elderly lady smiled and grinned slyly. "Well, since I've found you, my good friend Henrietta Wilson has a grandson, and I've heard he's very handsome. He's currently studying at Yale, and if you want, I could set a meeting between you both."

I tried not to laugh at Olivia's horrified expression.

"It's okay, I don't want to meet anyone at all. I'm fine."

The elderly woman smirked, and her eyes drifted to me. "Olivia, you didn't tell me you already had a boyfriend. What's your name, boy?"

I started choking while Olivia looked like she wanted to throw up. "Drake is not my boyfriend."

The elderly woman smirked again. "It's okay, Liv. I won't tell your brothers or your father. I'll keep your little secret." She cackled with glee before walking off.

I muttered, "That was awkward."

Olivia turned red when she looked at me again. "No shit, genius."

I scowled at her as she avoided my glare, clearly still embarrassed about the entire thing. Still, I couldn't help imagining her under me moaning, heck, screaming my name as I thrust into her.

"Stop staring at me like that!" I blinked as Olivia hissed at me with a blush on her face.

"Like what?"

Her green eyes were avoiding my blue ones while she played with her hair nervously. "Like you want to eat me. So knock it off!"

I grinned and remained silent as I turned my attention back to the meal. However, throughout the dinner, my eyes kept straying to her. *God, she was fucking gorgeous, and she fucking rejected me. This only made me want her even more. She was a candy treat that a little boy couldn't have just because he was punished.*

A grin crossed my face, I was determined to have her.

CHAPTER 5-THE OUTING

Olivia

The sound of someone knocking on my door woke me up. I loved my sleep, and no one gets in between that and me. Irritated that the knocking was not stopping, I growled angrily to myself and got out of bed before yanking the door open.

"What?"

"I should have known that you're not a morning person, sweetheart." His lazy voice drawled out. I looked up to see Drake leaning on my door frame. *God, he looked gorgeous.* His dark black hair was ruffled, and he looked extremely hot in a plain white V-neck shirt that showed his abs. I looked at his face to see him smirking. *Shit! He caught me checking him out!*

"What do you want? It's only around eight." I growled, irritated as I glanced at the clock. I crossed my arms and glared at him, waiting for an explanation.

He shrugged casually and shoved his hands into his pockets. "Your mother told me that you could give me a tour of the house. I didn't peg you for wearing oversized shirts to sleep, but I have to admit, you look hot."

I looked down at myself and cringed. *Great.* "Just stop talking and wipe that look off your face. I'll give you that damn tour in a moment. Just go get breakfast first." With that, I shut the door. Even though my door was closed, I could hear him laugh loudly. Why did he have to be so good looking but be such a jerk at the same time?

Life really, really wasn't fair.

Staring longingly at my bed, I sighed heavily before heading to my bathroom to shower. Once done with that, I slipped on some clothes and put on some lip gloss before heading down to the dining room for breakfast.

Nate immediately glanced up and did a double take. "Whoa, you're up early."

I rolled my eyes and replied grumpily, "Haha. Very funny."

I took a seat away from him and sat beside Penny, my niece. At that moment, Drake came down and roamed his eyes all over the seats until he saw me.

He smirked and headed towards me. "Good morning, sweetheart."

I felt shivers crawl up my spine when he called me 'sweetheart.' Damn, I was practically melting into my seat.

Forcing myself not to react, I ignored him and feigned nonchalance.

"It was a good morning before you woke me up." I snarled in response.

Drake laughed. "That's what you think. Though I know you're happy to see me here."

Giving him a fake smile, I quickly turned away from him, not wanting to deal with him anymore. It was way too early in the morning for this.

"Aunt Livvy, can I have ice cream? Mommy says no, but I want some."

I smiled at my niece and shook my head. "Sorry, Penny. Your mom would have my head if I did."

Penny pouted and munched on her cereal, her legs swung in the air as they were too short to reach the ground.

"I didn't know you were great with kids."

"I'm not that good with them," I said while patting Penny affectionately. I turned back to Drake, and he had a strange look on his face. He closed his eyes, and that annoying smirk appeared on his face once more.

"Anyway, since you're my tour guide, I want you to follow me back to my house to get my stuff."

"Why?" I pursed my lips. "And what makes you think I'll go with you?"

"First, I don't have my car here. It's back home. Second, Scott can't accompany me because he has to help plan the wedding and whatever comes with that. So, therefore, you're driving me back to my house." He shot me a devilish grin.

"Fine, whatever. You better be ready in ten minutes."

"You drive too slowly!"

"Okay! Fine!" I gritted my teeth and clenched my fingers around the steering wheel. I pressed my foot on the gas pedal.

"No! Not too fast! You're going to crash!" I sped faster and parked the car.

"Here! Drive the car. I refuse to drive it when you're bossing me around on how to drive."

I fumed at Drake, who merely blinked before shrugging. "Okay. Let's switch seats."

I balked at the audacity of him. He was so infuriating! I glared at him, got out of the car, and adjusted my skirt before slipping into the passenger seat.

His eyes roamed my legs appreciatively before he started the car. After a moment, I realized something. "This is the same speed I was going before you yelled at me about driving too fast!" I hissed at him, my fists clenching on my lap.

Drake laughed. "I know, I just wanted to drive your car."

I shut my eyes and bit my lip to prevent myself from exploding at Drake. I glanced at him to see him smirking smugly at me while driving.

My eyes trailed from his hands that were gripping the steering wheel to his forearm where his white T-shirt clung to his biceps like a second skin and where his black tattoo was.

Normally, I would find men with tattoos gross, considering the image that would come up in my mind were men in their fifties who would ride motorcycles and had beer bellies. But for Drake, I found it incredibly sexy.

I mentally slapped myself. *What the heck was wrong with me? I can't just go around ogling his tattoos.* I hurriedly glanced away while biting my lip.

"See something you like, sweetheart?"

I flushed and glanced at him. "No, and do stop calling me that."

"Calling you what? Sweetheart?"

"Yes. That."

Drake parked the car and got out to hold out the door for me.

"You don't seem like the type to have the chivalry gene," I muttered under my breath as I got out of the car when Drake helped me out. My fingers avoided any real body contact with him.

Drake snorted in response and shot me a smirk. "I do have it. I just want to show it off to you." He led me into his home, and I marveled at the interior design of the house.

"Feel free to sit around while I pack my things and have a shower. Unless you want to join me? My shower is big enough for two."

I shook my head vigorously. "No, thank you." I slid onto the couch, and Drake shrugged.

"Your loss, not mine."

I rolled my eyes and looked through some of the magazines he had lying on his sofa. Obviously, I avoided touching the Playboy copy he had.

What a pig.

Bored and wondering if his home matched his personality, I wandered around his living room. The penthouse was spacious enough. However, it was too perfect as if it lacked a personal feel to it. Also, I didn't spot any personal belongings that showed that Drake lived here.

Finally spotting a picture frame, I picked it up curiously. There was a smiling woman with two boys holding ice cream cones. Everyone in the photo was beaming happily, and I could see that the two boys resembled Scott and Drake greatly.

The woman was pretty in an understated way. Noting the vague similarities in their facial features, I guessed she had to be Scott and Drake's mother.

"She's pretty, isn't she?" I jumped and turned around. My hand was still holding the picture as Drake walked up towards me, drying his damp hair.

"Yeah. Is she your mother?"

Drake nodded in reply, his gaze still on the photo frame. I could see that his jaw was tense.

"Where's your dad?" I asked curiously, and immediately, I wished I hadn't spoken.

Drake's eyes hardened, and his mouth was set into a thin line. "Probably rotting in hell. Anyway, I'm done packing. Wanna have lunch?"

I blinked, confused by the sudden change of topic. "Yeah, sure," I replied casually, and Drake grinned. The change in his mood was giving me whiplash.

"So it's a date?"

I rolled my eyes. "No. It's not. I'm not interested in dating you."

Drake raised his eyebrow. "You wouldn't want to date all of this?" His right hand swept down from his head all the way to his torso, and I tried my very best not to look before snapping at him. My fingers gripped the edge of my blouse as I answered.

"No, I wouldn't. I've seen better." I crossed my arms and turned away, feigning boredom.

"Right. Sure. Only if you believe that, sweetheart, but both of us know better." He flashed me a smirk and walked off, leaving me scowling.

"So, where are we eating?" I asked as we drove to the fancier parts of New York.

Drake glanced at me teasingly. "Well, for our date, I'm taking you to a French restaurant around the corner. You do like French food, right?"

I frowned, confused. *French? How on earth does he know I like French food?* I narrowed my eyes. "First, we're not on a date. Second, how the heck do you know I like French food?"

"A little unicorn told me when I was dreaming." Drake blinked innocently at me before grinning.

I snorted and burst into laughter. "Very funny. No, seriously, who told you?"

"Wouldn't you like to know? Anyway, we're here."

I turned around and saw that we were at my favorite restaurant. Again, Drake held the door open for me, and I was glad I was appropriately dressed.

"Did Ellie tell you when the wedding will be?" he asked as his eyes scanned through the menu. His jean-clad thighs bumped against mine occasionally, sending little sparks of desire running through me. I bit my lip and discreetly moved my leg away.

"Uh, around Christmas season. Ellie said she wanted a Christmas wedding, even though I told her it was going to be cold."

"Christmas? That's like in five months! I'll be staying at your house for five months?" Drake sputtered in shock.

I raised my eyebrows. "I didn't know staying with my family is that terrible?"

Drake blinked. "Well, your brothers can be intimidating. Not that they scare me or anything."

"Right." I rolled my eyes and felt a tiny smile on my mouth before changing my expression.

From then on, conversation flowed easily until our food came. While eating, I could feel his blue eyes on me, and it was making me feel really flushed.

"Stop staring," I muttered, feeling embarrassed by the intensity of his gaze. I could already feel a blush gathering on my cheeks. I had never blushed, and this jerk in front of me is making me do that.

I chewed on my lower lip and glanced up from my meal to see Drake glancing at my lips before looking away. Our meal continued with light conversation and finally ended with Drake and I splitting the bill. I sternly refused to let him pay for my meal even though he insisted. In the end, I had gotten my way after arguing and loads of glaring.

"We should go now, or my brothers may suspect something. And, you're scared of them," I said. I smiled just a tiny bit as I teased.

"Sure, though your brothers won't suspect a single thing. They know very well that I don't date. I'm a player, and I enjoy it. So, don't get your hopes up, darling." He winked and stretched before turning away.

"Right. That's good. You're too annoying and egotistic, not to mention, a jerk."

Drake shrugged nonchalantly and grinned as he led me out of the restaurant. On the way back home, even though I know I should be relieved, I couldn't help but feel slightly disappointed.

CHAPTER 6-THE CHILDHOOD FRIEND

Olivia

I struggled to feed Phillip. He was frowning and refusing to open his mouth for the spoonful of carrots I wanted to give him.

"Phillip, open up. Aunty Livvy has a present for you on this spoon." I tried coaxing him. However, Lily only gave birth to him last year, so I didn't think he even understood what I'm talking about. Pursing my lips, I bit back a heavy sigh at my nephew's stubbornness.

"Thanks for feeding Phillip, Liv." Lily beamed at me as she entered her room with Penny. "Penny would be alright as long as she has bed rest. Her fever went down. Now all she has to do is sleep." Lily laid her five-year-old daughter on the bed and went to take the spoon and the jar of baby food from me.

"That's great. It's really weird to see Penny so… quiet." I peered at the five-year-old, who was almost an exact replica of Lily.

Lily laughed and fed Phillip, who now opened his mouth eagerly.

I glared at Phillip. He wouldn't even budge when I tried to feed him. *That little brat. I was the best aunt he had! Ellie didn't count.*

Lily was prattling to me about Penny when Parker burst into the room. Immediately, Lily brightened and went towards him. I looked away and grimaced when they kissed each other.

"Hey, Liv." Parker greeted me, and I gave an awkward wave.

"You're back home early from Los Angeles. I thought you were coming back this Wednesday?" Lily asked as Parker reached for Phillip and cradled him. While my niece was a carbon copy of her mother, my nephew Phillip, on the other hand, was a miniature version of his dad.

"Yeah, but something came up with my dad and Vincent."

"What happened? Did they have an argument?"

Vincent was Parker's younger brother and had been causing problems for Parker's dad. Vincent didn't want to work in the family company but wanted to be a freelance photographer instead.

Parker nodded. "Yeah. Dad kicked Vincent out of the house and cut off all of Vincent's credit cards." Lily frowned while I listened with interest. It was slightly funny to hear a twenty-six-year-old man be treated like a teenager.

"So, where's your brother going to stay?" Lily asked worriedly, took Phillip from Parker, and continued feeding him.

Parker rubbed his neck sheepishly. "I kinda invited him to stay here, if it's okay with your parents."

Lily beamed. "They'll be fine with it. Besides, they treat Vincent and you as their own. We're family after all."

Parker shrugged, and I was excited.

Vincent had been one of my best friends when we were younger, but I had not seen him much when his father had shipped him off to boarding school. He had also been unable to come to Parker and Lily's wedding as he was stranded in some rural town in Mexico.

"So, when's Vincent arriving?" Lily asked as she gave Philip a stern glare when he spat some of his food out. I watched on with mild disgust at the sight of the mashed baby food trailing down Philip's bib.

"Um, he's here already. He's outside our room," Parker said casually as he walked over to Penny. "Is she feeling better?"

Lily stared astounded at Parker before slapping his arm. "You could have said that earlier. Bring your brother in!" Lily reprimanded before answering Parker's question. "And yes, the doctor said she needs bed rest. Loads of it."

Lily turned away and opened the door with Phillip in her arms.

A man I vaguely recognized grinned at Lily. "Hey, Lily. Is that my nephew?"

My jaw dropped. *That man was Vincent? Holy shit.* The scrawny, thin boy I remembered is now a tall, muscular man.

While I was still marveling at the changes of my childhood friend, Lily had already invited him into their suite.

His eyes landed on me and widened. "Olive?"

I broke into a wide grin. I hadn't heard that nickname for a long time. "Hey, Vincent!" I grinned as he stalked towards me. His arms stretched and pulled me into a hug.

"Oh wow, you look fantastic." Vincent grinned, his green eyes beaming happily at me.

"You look great too."

Vincent grinned at me before turning to Parker. "So, where am I going to sleep?"

Lily chewed on her lip. "Um, the guest room on the second level. Livvy, take him there. I have to watch over Penny before she has another fever."

"So, how have you been? I have not heard from you in years." I grinned at Vincent and pulled him along.

"Heck yes. It's been great traveling here and there until this. But enough about that, any boyfriends?"

At that question, I turned around, glared at him, and played with my fingers against my arm. "You too? Why is everyone asking me that? My dad, my brothers, Ellie, and now you. Fantastic!"

Vincent grinned and ran his fingers through his hair. "Right, sorry. Where's Tristan?"

"I don't know. You'll be attending Ellie's wedding, right?"

"Yeah, wouldn't miss it. So where am I sleeping again? I'm exhausted."

"You sound exactly like a baby, you know that?"

Vincent raised an eyebrow, and a smirk crossed his lips. "Sure. So, I'm serious, any boyfriends?" I could feel him watching me, and I knew he was waiting impatiently for an answer.

I let out a heavy sigh and barely spared him a glance. "No. I don't have one. Anyway, this is your room." I gestured him to open the door. The room that he was staying in was a few doors down from Drake's. Drake wasn't around as he had to go with Scott for suit fittings for the best man tux.

I hadn't seen Drake since that little lunch thing with him at the restaurant, and I wasn't curious about what he had been up to for the past two weeks. Nope. I was not curious at all. I had been busy helping with wedding preparations. I didn't understand why so many flowers were needed in a wedding until it felt like I was visiting a botanic garden.

Ellie was that bad in planning her wedding.

"So what about you? Any girlfriends?"

"Nope. I'm interested in one, but she doesn't like me back." Vincent grinned, his eyes sparkling with glee before he glanced away.

"Not interested in you? She must be blind." I mocked Vincent, and he scowled at me playfully before poking me in the waist with one of his fingers.

"She certainly is not to see this." He gestured towards himself, and I rolled my eyes. It seems that almost every good-looking guy is about their looks.

I rolled my eyes and went out of the room with him following me.

He suddenly grabbed me, backed me against the wall, and stared at me intensely. "Would you be interested in me?"

I blinked and balked at his words. Vincent was like another brother to me, and the image of him running around nude was still fresh in my mind just like eighteen years ago.

"I—"

I was interrupted by Drake pulling Vincent off me.

"Who the heck are you?" Drake demanded Vincent.

Vincent in return replied coolly, "No. Who the heck are you?"

I watched wide-eyed as the two men stared each other down.

"I'm Drake Henderson, Ellie's brother-in-law. Who are you?"

Vincent raised his eyebrows. "I'm Vincent Forrer, a family friend and…" Vincent pulled me towards him and wrapped an arm around my shoulders. "… Olivia's childhood best friend."

Drake narrowed his eyes at us, his fists clenching up. Vincent was tense as he stiffened against me.

What was with men thinking that everything could be solved with fists? Math equations can't be solved with fists, and tense, awkward confrontations shouldn't be solved with a fight too.

I knew I had to intervene. I pushed Vincent away and stepped between them. "Drake, cut it out. This is my best friend, Vincent. He's Parker's brother. Vincent, this is Drake. His older brother is Scott, Ellie's fiancé. And if you hit Drake, you'll suffer the wrath of Ellie."

Vincent laughed. "Who said I'll hit him? There's no way in hell I'll be suffering any wrath, especially from Ellie. Not after the last time."

Drake watched us with narrowed eyes and stalked off angrily, leaving me staring at his retreating form.

What crawled up his ass today?

CHAPTER 7-THE FIRST KISS

Olivia

I glanced nervously at the floor, embarrassed beyond relief. Drake had been leaving me in a hot mess ever since we got here — here as in some bridal shop where we have to do our fittings. I grasped the hem of my dress tightly and fidgeted slightly as I resisted throwing Drake dark looks.

He had been leaving lingering touches on my thighs, waist, and my back. I was absolutely a hundred percent sure that he was doing all of this on purpose. And, I was melting. I bit my lip as Drake watched me lustfully with a sexy smirk on his face as the seamstress adjusted the size of my dress.

I really cursed Ellie for choosing this dress. It was ridiculous. The dress was tight, short, and slightly low-cut, and it was red. I, for one, thought it was really inappropriate for a bridesmaid dress. Furthermore, it was all the more reason for Drake to look at me as if I was some racing car he coveted.

"Got to say, you look really good."

I blushed profusely as Drake's eyes were practically devouring me and I felt really conscious, but I forced myself to stare back at him evenly. I was not going to give him the satisfaction of him to get under my skin.

"Shut up!" I bit out at him and received a smug grin in return.

When the seamstress stepped away from me, Drake took her place, and his hands rested on my waist. I could feel the warm heat from his hand all the way to my toes. His hot breath fanned across my neck, making goosebumps appear.

"Move away from me," I ordered weakly before growling at him.

Drake chuckled and went back to his seat. He had already tried his tux, and I almost drooled. He looked ruggedly handsome even though he was dressed in a form-fitting tux.

"There. Your dress is done." The seamstress dismissed me with a wave of her hand, and I stepped down from the small platform.

"Thank you," I told her.

"Wanna get a drink or something?" Drake asked lazily as he stood up.

"Alright."

We walked to a nearby cafe, and once we were seated, "Did you know that your childhood bestie is in love with you?" he questioned mockingly.

I blinked and frowned before shooting him a skeptical glance. "No, he isn't. Vincent likes someone else."

Drake shook his head knowingly. "He does, but it's not who you think."

I rolled my eyes. "You're kidding. Wait, why am I even listening to you? You don't even know Vincent. I do. He's been my friend since kindergarten." I pointed out before sipping my glass of iced tea.

Drake shrugged and stretched back in his seat. "He does. I'm a guy."

"Clearly," I replied dryly before leaning back in my chair, and he shot me a flat look.

"And because of that, I obviously know what he's thinking," Drake said nonchalantly as he examined the tip of his fingers.

"Even if he does and asks me out on a date, I wouldn't accept. Vincent is just a friend. Nothing more, nothing less. But like I said earlier, he doesn't have any interest in me. Also, if we were talking about a completely different scenario, the likely chance of me accepting his date would be higher than yours."

Drake narrowed his eyes at me and leaned in closer. "At least, if I take you out on one, it'll be better than his."

"What makes you so sure that it'll be better?" I raised my eyebrow.

Drake smirked charmingly at me but didn't bother elaborating. As I sipped on my iced tea, I studied Drake, concluding that there was certainly a reason why he was a player. I thought, there must have been something that happened between his parents. I could even remember the hate when Drake spoke about his father.

"You done? Scott just called. Ellie's in a foul mood and needs you."

I paled. Ellie was in a foul mood? Good god. "Okay, let's go."

Drake stood up and led me to his car. I opened the car door before he could and slid in.

"How am I ever going to impress you if you don't let me?"

"Just drive." I snapped, and Drake still had the audacity to laugh. Now would be a very good time to slam my fist into his mouth.

"What's the big fuss if Ellie has a temper? Won't she just throw a mere tantrum?"

I pursed my lips. "When Ellie has a temper, her tantrum gets really, really destructive. You do not want her to be upset with you."

"I don't think it's that bad," Drake said as we entered the house to see Ellie shrieking at Scott, who looked totally lost.

"I told you that I don't give a damn! Stop apologizing!" She threw a cup onto the floor and Scott flinched as the porcelain teacup shattered into pieces as he tried to make his way towards his distraught fiancée.

"You can say, 'How's life?' to any of your ex-girlfriends and I don't care! Why don't you also say you wanna fuck any of them? Fucking go ahead, I won't stop you!" Again, she threw a champagne bottle onto the ground.

"Just get out!" She grabbed a cushion and threw it at Scott.

"I take it back. She fucking scares me," Drake muttered under his breath, but I ignored him.

"Ellie, what did he do?" Ellie turned to me, and her eyes started watering. She ran towards me and sobbed.

"Scott, he didn't e-even—" Ellie broke off with another sob. I patted her arm comfortingly and led her to my room.

"Okay, we're alone now. You can share what happened."

Ellie's lower lip trembled. "We were having lunch, and there was this girl who was his ex-girlfriend. She just sat next to him and started rubbing all over him, and he didn't say or do a thing! I even had to introduce myself, and the only thing he did was ask her how was life!"

I blinked as Ellie shrieked the last part.

"I mean, he could at least say I was his fiancée, but he didn't, and it hurt. The worst part was that he didn't seem to mind his ex-girlfriend rubbing all over him."

I glanced sympathetically at Ellie and pulled her into a hug as she hiccupped and sobbed. "It's alright, Ellie. I think you should let Scott explain himself and not jump to conclusions. He loves you, remember?" I consoled and patted her arm gently.

Ellie nodded slowly, and I handed her a tissue. "Okay, you're right. I'll go to him now." Ellie exited my room, and I followed her. Ellie was the most emotional one in our family. Her emotions can turn from one to another in just a minute or less. I was slightly thankful that I had not inherited that gene from anyone.

"You're not like Ellie, right?"

I glanced at Drake and groaned, he was waiting for me outside my room, leaning on the wall. "No, I'm not that emotional. It's the wedding jitters. What are you doing here?"

"That's a relief." He shrugged and slid his hands into his pockets.

I frowned in confusion. "Why?"

Drake shrugged and gave me a sexy grin as he neared me. "Because I'm gonna do this."

"Do wha…?" I was cut off when Drake's lips landed on mine. His mouth tasted of coffee. The kiss was demanding, rough, and different from every kiss I ever had. His lips moved against mine quickly. Desire was racing across my nerves, and I was succumbing quickly to the kiss. I kissed Drake back with the same urgency, my hands tangled in his dark hair, and I loved the silky feeling of it in my hands.

His lips were soft yet firm. His tongue slipped into my mouth and explored every crevice. While his mouth was sensually assaulting mine, his hands roamed my back and landed on my butt, and I was embarrassed to say that I moaned… loudly.

Drake chuckled huskily against my lips and pulled away. "Does this answer your question?"

I blinked and asked breathlessly, "What question?"

"You asked what would make my date with you better than Vincent's. I hope the kiss answered your question," he huskily answered and walked off.

I blinked, too lost for words. That was undoubtedly the best kiss I ever had.

CHAPTER 8-THE HOSPITAL

Olivia

Holy shit. I breathed silently and leaned against the wall. My lips were still tingling. I placed my fingers on my lips and gasped. They felt really tender and swollen, and I was pretty sure if I looked into the mirror, I would see that they were bright red.

Drake kissed me. He bloody kissed me! And I enjoyed it. I cringed as I recalled how I had moaned loudly. *Damn it.* Drake managed to get under my skin again.

I knew I was attracted to him, but did he have to kiss me? Now, I was going to have a hard time getting him out of my mind especially since the kiss was mindblowing. It was better than any kiss I've ever had.

How did Drake learn to kiss like that? I snorted. *Right, he was a womanizer. How could I forget? There would be no future for Drake and me, anyway. 'Once a player, always a player.' That was the saying, wasn't it?*

How was I going to forget a kiss like that? It was earth-shatteringly amazing.

"Livvy, are you okay?" my mom asked worriedly as she walked towards me. It seemed like she was back from one of her many honeymoons with my dad.

I nodded my head vigorously. "Yeah, I'm fine."

My mom frowned. "Then why are you standing outside the door like you're going to faint?"

"I-I was just thinking about something."

My mum raised an eyebrow and grimaced. "Oh, I see," my mom murmured before bending over and clutching her head.

My eyes widened, and I ran towards her. "Mum, are you okay? What's happening?"

My mum paled and fainted. I gasped and caught her as she fell.

"Dad!" I yelled as loud as I could.

"What is it? Shit, what the heck happened?" My dad panicked when he saw my mother's motionless body on the floor.

"I don't know. She was talking, and suddenly, she fainted before collapsing on the floor," I said tearfully.

"Ria, Ria! Wake up, wake up! Shit. Damn it! Livvy, call the ambulance now!"

I nodded trembling, and with my shaky fingers, I dialed for an ambulance while my dad cradled her and picked her up.

The ambulance came, and I stood silently as my dad yelled at the paramedics who were trying to appease him and took my mom from him. I stared frozenly at my mother's unmoving body. My dad was now standing beside her and held her hand tightly while begging her to wake up.

I bit my lip worriedly. My mom was everything to me. She was there every time I got my heart broken, at every piano recital, and every dance competition. Gazing forlornly at my mom, I clutched her other hand tightly. I couldn't live without my mom. My mom was my confidant, she was my source of comfort, and she was always there for me.

The minute we reached the hospital, the paramedics rushed my mom off. My dad slumped onto one of the plastic seats.

"Livvy, call your siblings." I nodded.

It seemed like an hour had passed after I called my siblings, informing them about what was going on when really it was about a few minutes. Dad has been pacing nervously in the hallway.

"Livvy! What happened? Where's mom?" I glanced up to see Lily rushing over to us with Phillip in her arms while Parker followed behind her with Penny.

"She fainted at home," I replied, still in shock.

Lily nodded slowly and murmured softly to me, "How's dad?"

"He's very quiet. I don't want to know what would happen to him if anything happened to mom."

Lily nodded in agreement and sat down.

"Where's mom? What happened?" Ellie ran to us with Scott and Drake behind her.

"She fainted at home," Lily answered as she rocked Phillip.

"She fainted?" Ellie shrieked, and tears welled up in her eyes. Scott patted her comfortingly as she sobbed on him. Watching them, I guessed both had made up already.

Somehow, I was too numb to feel or react when Drake came. My mind was set on my mom. Nothing else mattered to me, not even Drake's kiss.

"Hey, are you okay?" I glanced up at Drake to see him looking at me concerned.

"Yeah, I'm fine."

Drake sat down beside me and remained silent.

"I want to know where my mother is!" Nate's voice could be heard as he bellowed out at a nurse while my remaining two brothers rushed towards us worriedly.

The door opened, and a doctor stepped out. Immediately, my dad stood up. "Is she okay?"

"Are you related to her?"

My dad glared at the doctor and snapped. "I'm her bloody husband!"

The doctor shot him a disapproving look before continuing, "Yes she is okay. Your wife is just suffering from severe dehydration. That's how she fainted. She's very weak and requires more fluids and bed rest."

All of us breathed out a sigh of relief. My body relaxed slightly, and the tension in my chest ceased at the bit of news.

"Can I see her now?" my dad asked and went in without waiting for the doctor's response. All of us went into the room. I watched my mom brighten up as she spotted us.

I bit my lip anxiously. Even though the doctor said my mom would be fine, I was still worried about her. She was unusually pale and frail looking.

"I knew I shouldn't have taken you to Hawaii. The weather there is way too hot," My dad muttered angrily to himself.

"It was my fault. I didn't keep out of the shade most of the time, and I really enjoyed it." My mom frowned and took his hand gently.

A smile creased my dad's face as he held onto her hand tightly. Lily and Ellie were fussing over mom. Parker had left to get drinks for everyone, and my brothers were prodding the doctor for more details and questions.

I sighed heavily as I observed my parents.

"I really want the kind of love my parents had."

"Why would you want that?" My head snapped up to see Drake looking down at me.

I blinked. I didn't know I had spoken my thoughts out loud. "Why wouldn't I want that?"

Drake's expression hardened. "Why would you want that? It's a weakness that can be used and exploited against you."

My mouth dropped wide open in shock. "So, you're saying that my parents will turn against each other?" I sputtered in disbelief.

"Not saying it will. Just saying it could happen," Drake said with his jaw clenched.

"What happened to you, Drake?" I definitely knew something horrible must have happened to him to make him so against love.

Drake tensed and stiffened as if he didn't want to reveal too much of himself. "Nothing. It is none of your concern, Olive." He walked out. It seemed that the more I got to know Drake, the more curious I got about him.

CHAPTER 9-THE CONTEMPLATION

Drake

I couldn't get that kiss out of my mind. The kiss I've shared with Olivia. I had no fucking clue. I have kissed many women before, but this particular kiss stood out the most. Why? I didn't know. I rubbed at my face with agitation before giving up.

Olivia's face came into my mind. Her eyes were glazed over, red lips parted and swollen. That thought alone made all blood rush south.

"Shit!" I glared down at my crotch. *I really do not need this now.*

I grabbed a jacket and left the Ford's mansion. I needed to let off some steam, and I knew where to do it.

Where else other than the race tracks where all I would think about is driving through the race course?

"Heading out, Mr. Henderson?" I turned to see Ford's butler peering at me.

I ran my hand through my hair. "Yeah."

"Have a good day then, Mr. Henderson." I nodded at Edward and left. I started driving, and Olivia crept into my mind again.

"Dammit!" I cursed as I pressed harder on the gas pedal. Soon, I reached the place I knew would take my mind off her.

"Henderson! Where the hell have you been? You were supposed to be here four hours earlier."

I raised my eyebrows at Rick and shrugged. "I forgot."

"Where have you been?"

"Scott's getting married, and I'm the best man, so things have been really hectic."

"He's getting married? To whom?"

"Elena Ford," I answered as I slipped into my driving suit.

"Elena Ford? Wow." Rick frowned as he shrugged before handing me my helmet. I turned and gave Rick a grin. Rick's expression was priceless. "Wait, your brother is marrying *the* Elena Ford?"

"Yeah," I replied as I zipped up my suit before grabbing a bottle of water.

"They have like six kids, don't they? Are they those people with sticks shoved up their ass?" Rick questioned curiously.

I frowned. The Fords were pretty down to earth, and they didn't let their money get to their heads. "No, they're pretty cool." I slid into my car and shut the door.

Rick raised his eyebrows and gave me a stern glare. "Make sure you come back here after twenty. We still have to go through your upcoming races in two months."

"Yeah, yeah. I know." I waved him off. Sometimes, I just wished I was back to illegal street racing. I didn't have to answer to anyone back then. Well, except to my boss, but he was pretty relaxed.

Seeing that the conversation was going nowhere, Rick walked off. I grinned to myself and started the engine. The engine roared to life, and I flexed my fingers and drummed them impatiently on the steering wheel.

As I drove several rounds around the race track, I could feel the wind rushing against my ears through the helmet. I loved racing. It helped keep me sane in my screwed up life. Finally, Rick flagged me down to stop. Reluctantly, I pulled to a stop and got out.

"Sorry to interrupt, but we have a big race in about two months. And as usual, I have to go through the procedures and more."

"Not again." I let out a loud grunt while Rick grinned.

Fucking sadistic bastard.

As we were sitting down, I couldn't help thinking about taking Olivia on one of the office chairs I was sitting on.

"Drake!"

I blinked up at Rick, who was getting annoyed. "Where were you? I've been calling you for the past three minutes. You better not be thinking of some hooker."

I glared at Rick. "She's not a hooker." *Shit, I slipped up.*

Rick raised an eyebrow. "She? You never talked about a *she* before." Usually, when Rick made a comment about some blonde airhead, I'll laugh about it. "Must be some girl, huh?"

"You have no idea," I muttered before cracking my knuckles. It was a habit that Rick hated as he claimed that the sound bothered him. True enough, Rick shuddered before shooting a glare in my direction.

"So, who's she?"

"Olivia Ford."

"Olivia Ford? Is she Elena Ford's sister? Whoa, your game's gone down. Two women rejected you? That's a record-breaking event."

"My game has not gone down, the air stewardess and Oliva Ford is one and the same."

Rick blinked and roared out laughing. "Ha! The great Drake Henderson has finally met his match!"

"Are you done? If all I'm here is to be made fun of, I'm going." I scowled before slumping back in my chair.

Rick raised his hands in surrender. "Okay, I'll drop it."

At that moment, my cell phone rang. I groaned and answered with a gruff hello.

"Drake, I'm at the airport here in New York. Could you pick me up?" My mother called, and I could hear the sounds from the traffic in the background.

I sat up straight on my chair and frowned. "What do you mean you're here? Aren't you in Hawaii?"

"I was until Scott called to tell me he was getting married."

I hurriedly got out of the chair, grabbed my jacket, and mouthed to Rick that I needed to go. "I'll be there quick. Don't stand for too long."

Immediately, I drove off to the airport, and as I arrived, I spotted my mother with her luggage in her hand.

My mother beamed at me and kissed my cheek. "Hi, hon."

"Hey mom, did Scott say where you will be staying?" I grinned at her and ran my fingers through my hair.

"Yes, at his fiancée's house because she wanted to meet me. When will you settle down like your brother? You need someone to love you and vice versa. And, I am tired of seeing you in those trashy magazines." My mom raised her eyebrows before crossing her arms. Disapproval was practically dripping from her every pore.

I rolled my eyes. "Where's the fun in that?"

My mom shot me a sad smile. "You shouldn't let what happened to me affect you."

I clenched my jaw and looked away. "Come, let's go meet Ellie."

"Drake, please don't let what happened in the past affect your future. Mine may have turned out the way no one wanted, but you—"

"Mom, stop," I said sharply. My mother bit her lip, nodded, and turned her head towards the window, leaving the scar on her left cheek clear for me to see. Guilt started to form in the pit of my stomach. "I'm sorry. It's just I don't want to talk about it."

My mom smiled gently at me. "It's alright, hon."

Could my mother be right? Should I just move on from what happened in the past? Could I actually find happiness like Scott and Rick?

"So tell me, what's your brother's fiancée like? From your perspective."

"She's very bubbly but emotional."

My mom blinked and laughed affectionately. "She must have been keeping Scott on his toes, hasn't she?"

My mind flashed to the image of Ellie during one of her tempers while my brother looked lost. "Yeah, she does. We're here."

"Wow!" My mom glanced and gaped at the looming mansion.

I laughed and stopped the car to see Scott and Ellie. I guessed that my mother had called my brother to let him know that she was arriving.

"Hello, Mrs. Henderson! I'm Elena, but please call me Ellie! It's a pleasure to meet you!"

Scott and I tensed when Ellie called our mother 'Mrs. Henderson.'

My mom broke out into a grin and hugged Ellie. "I go by Ms. Reed now but call me Kaitlyn."

Ellie bit her lip and squealed excitedly. "Okay. Come, let's go in! Scott, get your mom's luggage."

I followed after them to see Olivia chasing Phillip. "Phillip! Get back here now." I guess she must not have seen me because she crashed right into me. "Shit! I'm so sorry. Oh, it's just you."

"Carry!" I felt a tugging on my jeans to see Phillip pulling them. I was about to pick him up when Olivia snatched him away. Her nose went up in the air the minute she spotted me.

"Phillip! You're not allowed to talk to Drake. He's a mean person." She scooped him up, and Phillip immediately scrunched up his nose and tears started running down his cheeks.

Olivia's eyes grew round, and she started panicking. I smirked, took Phillip from her, and placed him on my shoulders.

Instantly, Phillip quieted down, and Olivia shot Phillip a glare. "Brat," she muttered under her breath.

I chuckled, and she pouted. "Come on, Phillip, don't you like Aunt Livvy?"

Phillip shook his head, and I laughed at Olivia's annoyed expression. I put Phillip on the ground, and he ran off as fast his chubby toddler legs could. Finally, we were alone.

She was about to leave when I grabbed her arm. "Wait. We have to talk."

She turned towards me, confusion marring her features. "What's there to talk about? I don't really particularly like you. You just want to sleep with me, and I'm going to say no. So I don't think we have to talk, considering there's nothing to say."

She was gorgeous when she was annoyed. That was for sure. I rubbed the back of my neck and said, "Look, Olivia, I just— I want us to start over. We got off on the wrong foot. I want to ask you out." *There, I said it. This would be the first time I ever asked a girl out.*

Olivia scrutinized me carefully. Her head was cocked to one side, leaving her golden hair which was bunched into a ponytail lying over her bare shoulders.

She frowned and pursed her lips before saying, "No."

CHAPTER 10-THE CHANGE OF HEART

Olivia

"Look, Olivia, I just— I want us to start over. We got off on the wrong foot. I want to ask you out."

I couldn't be more shocked, to say the least. I tilted my head to the side and squinted my eyes at Drake. He seemed sincere, but he wanted to ask me out? Ha! The biggest womanizer in the country just suddenly converted into a gentleman?

Ha! Too bad! Well, I had to give Drake some credit. He wasn't checking me out at all. He was just looking into my eyes sincerely. Well, I, Olivia Ford had enough of dating jerks, cheaters, and gold-digging assholes.

"No."

"No?" Drake sputtered.

"Yeah, no. I don't believe a playboy can just be converted to a one-woman guy. So, yeah." I walked off, leaving Drake, to find Ellie.

I entered the lounge to find her and Scott chatting with the woman that Drake brought. "Liv, look! Scott's mom is here!"

The woman turned around, and it was indeed the same woman that I had seen in the photograph in Drake's apartment.

"Hi, you must be Olivia. Ellie has told me about her many siblings. You can call me Kaitlyn."

I gave a small smile and took Phillip into my lap, who was wriggling around in Ellie's arms. Kaitlyn was really pretty, but there was a long, jagged scar on her left cheek as if someone had slashed her with a knife. Of course, I knew better not to ask about sensitive stuff like that, so I kept my mouth shut.

"Aunt Livvy, I'm hungry."

I sighed. "Okay."

I was about to stand when Ellie stood up. "I'll grab it! You can talk to Kaitlyn. Come, Scott!" She dragged Scott along with her and Phillip in her arms.

That sneak! Did she think I did not know what she was planning? Making me talk to Drake's mother. It's another one of her stupid matchmaking plans! I gritted my teeth and frantically thought of a way out of this mess.

"So, Olivia, how old are you? You are the youngest, right?"

"I'm twenty-three. It does kinda suck to be the youngest, though," I said while shifting on the red suede chair awkwardly.

"Ah, I get it. I have four older brothers. So how long have you known Drake?"

My head snapped up to meet her eyes, and I stammered. "Um, recently?"

Kaitlyn laughed. "You can say whatever you want about my sons. They can be a jerk or a playboy to women. It's a wonder how Scott even got someone like Ellie to marry him."

I laughed, and Phillip came into the room with a box of crackers in his hand. I placed him on my lap as Kaitlyn said, "I know it's wrong to eavesdrop, but it's the first time I've ever heard Drake ask a woman out and gets turned down on the first time."

My face flushed in response. *God! Could this get any more embarrassing? Drake and I weren't even friends for crying out loud! But Drake had never asked a girl out before? But he had asked me out...*

"Um. I had enough bad relationships, so I'm trying to stay out of any," I said truthfully and fiddled with the hem of my shirt. Kaitlyn smiled, and I could see the similar traits that Drake shared with her—the same kind of eyes, the same black hair, and the dimple on the right cheek.

"Well, I think you should say yes, not because he's my son but because Drake thinks love is pointless, and he is actually interested for the first time. Not just for sex but for something more."

"What made Drake think that love is a terrible thing?" I asked curiously. This was not the first time I had heard of Drake's twisted view of love.

Kaitlyn sighed, and her hand traced unconsciously across the scar on her cheek. "Our family wasn't this messed up. But when, uh, my ex-husband Ted went to jail, everything just fell apart. Fortunately, Scott didn't have the same beliefs as Drake."

I bit my lip. It wasn't the whole story I was looking for, but I guessed it was good enough. "Oh, um, I'm really sorry."

Kaitlyn bit her lip and shrugged. "It's okay. It's all in the past. So, why don't you give Drake a chance? Just one date."

I remained quiet and stroked Phillip's dark curly hair.

"I'm just saying. Please, think about it? I'm sorry if I come off as demanding, but I just want to see my son happy."

"I understand. I don't blame you."

Kaitlyn smiled at me.

"Hey, mom, Ellie's mom wants to meet you, but she'll be slightly late." Scott strolled into the room just as we finished speaking.

Kaitlyn smiled brightly. "It's okay." And she launched into a conversation with Ellie and Scott about the upcoming nuptials. It was when I decided to leave along with Phillip.

Thinking back to what Kaitlyn had said, I didn't know if I should accept Drake's offer or not anymore. Before, I would never ever go on a date with a womanizer. But understanding why Drake was the way he was, I was having second thoughts. It didn't help that I was actually interested, not that I wanted anyone to know that.

Should I give it a go or not?

"Olivia!" Drake appeared in front of me frowning while looking at me pleadingly.

Oh, why did he have to be so good-looking? I mean, I don't mind turning down a not so good-looking Drake. But, the actual Drake Henderson was hot with a capital 'H'!

I stopped and stared back uncertainly.

"Look, I'm serious about asking you out. At least, agree to this date, and if you don't like it, I won't harass you for it anymore. Just—"

And without thinking, I said, "Yes."

CHAPTER 11-THE DATE IN MCDONALD'S

Olivia

"Just agree, and it'll be the best date of your life. Wait, you said yes?" Drake blinked in surprise and shock.

"Yes. I did," I said casually.

"Great. I'll pick you up at six. Dress warmly."

I watched him walk off, and I couldn't help my eyes stray to his ass. *Why did those jeans have to make his butt look so good? It wasn't fair. It really wasn't.*

I went to Lily's room to pass Phillip back to her and headed to my room to get ready. I grabbed my favorite pair of jeans, and an emerald green knitted top before pairing them with boots.

After a long nice luxurious bath, I started to dress, and around six, there were three consecutive knocks. "Hey, you're—"

"Wanna hang out tonight? I didn't get to hang around with you much. My dad and I made a deal, and I'll be heading back to New York City by next week," Vincent casually asked as he leaned against the doorframe.

"Wow! That's great, but I'm actually heading out."

The conversation between Drake and me about Vincent's feelings for me surfaced into my mind, and I could feel an awkward tension rise. I fidgeted slightly from how uncomfortable I was getting.

"Oh, where are you going? Can I tag along?" Vincent grinned charmingly though it didn't make my heart race when Drake did it.

"Um, I'm actually going on a date." I bit my lip, waiting for the reactions I would get from Vincent if what Drake had told me about Vincent liking me was true.

"With who?" *Oh god! Drake was right!* Vincent's eyes were narrowed, and his body was tense. "Livvy, with who?" he questioned impatiently.

"She's going out with me," Drake answered nonchalantly with his hands in his pockets as he walked towards us. Normally, any girl would be totally flattered by the fact that two men would be fighting for her. Well, for me, I was flattered, but I wanted this confrontation to end. *I wasn't one for big blow-ups.*

"With you? Olivia, why would you choose some womanizer?"

I winced inwardly. "I—"

"The said womanizer is taking Olivia for *our* date now." Drake interrupted me and emphasized the word "our." He wrapped an arm around my waist, gripped my hips possessively, and led us away.

"I'm really sorry for Vincent's attitude," I said quietly.

Drake gave me a lazy grin and shrugged nonchalantly. "It's alright, and have I mentioned you look beautiful?" He looked at me with his smoldering blue eyes, and I blushed.

I cleared my throat and changed the topic. "So, where are you taking me?"

"Wouldn't you like to know." Drake smirked.

I rolled my eyes and mumbled. "Typical."

Drake peered behind me at the empty hallway before pushing me against the wall and slamming his lips against mine. His mouth moved urgently against mine, tongue sought entrance, and hands gripped tightly around my waist.

"Open up for me," Drake huskily demanded to which I responded by pressing my lips even more firmly to tease him. Drake growled and ground his arousal against me, making me gasp in shock. *God, he felt huge.*

Immediately, Drake's tongue slipped into my mouth, and he kissed me hungrily. My hands found their way to Drake's hair, and I ran my fingers through it, enjoying the silky feeling. He started trailing kisses down my neck, nibbling lightly as he went down to the area between my neck and my shoulders. As he bit on a particular area on my neck, I let out a loud breathy moan.

I could feel Drake smirking against my neck as he started sucking and nibbling on that area with his hands still on my ass.

"Ahem."

I gasped loudly and shoved Drake off me.

My heart was racing wildly as I saw Tristan staring at us in disgust.

"Livvy, please do not show PDA in front of me. You're my little sister. I don't want to lose any of my meals just because both of you can't keep your hormones in check."

I rolled my eyes and bit my lip worriedly. "Please don't tell anyone."

Tristan shrugged. "I wasn't going to. I won't take part in World War Three."

With that, Tristan walked on, shooting Drake a little glare, but thankfully, he had no intention of beating Drake up. I glanced up at Drake to see him smirking satisfactorily at me.

"What?" Drake shook his head and wrapped his arm around my waist.

"Nothing, let's go."

Alright, that's the third time someone has given me a strange glance before walking off.

Now, Drake was taking me for dinner, and we were walking towards the restaurant. At least, the restaurant was elegant but casual.

"Um, excuse me, do you need a concealer?"

I shot a confused glance at the teenager. "Uh, what? No, thanks." Make that four people now.

"Reservation under Henderson," Drake said to the hostess. The hostess shot me a strange look before leading us off.

"Drake, is there anything wrong with my attire?"

Drake raked me up from top to toe before shooting me a lustful look. "No. In fact, you look so fucking hot."

I was kinda thankful that the restaurant was dim so that Drake couldn't see me blush.

As we sat down, I noticed a man staring at me, and he gave Drake a grin which Drake returned with a wink.

Okay, that's it. I'm going to the washroom. I peered into the mirror, and my eyes widened.

Oh, my God! I'm so going to kill Drake. There was a giant purple hickey on my neck where I couldn't hide it. No wonder so many people have given me strange looks and one even offered a concealer!

I growled and covered the hickey with my hair. *Drake was so going to get it from me.* I stalked out of the washroom furiously and glared at Drake, who was smirking at me.

"You are such an asshole, Henderson!" I hissed.

Drake laughed and shrugged. "I was just staking my claim on you."

"I am not a possession!" My anger spiked even higher as I growled.

"I know, but men would be hitting on you constantly if *my* mark was not there."

I rolled my eyes. "What are you talking about?"

Drake leaned forward and stared at me intensely. "Of course, you don't see it. You're gorgeous, and you give off an attitude that you don't seem to care about it. You also have confidence, and that's a turn on for most males."

I was left speechless. I mean, well, how do you even respond to that?

"I—" I cut myself off when I noticed two familiar figures head into the restaurant. *Shit!* "Drake, get your head down and slowly head out of the restaurant when I say so."

Drake frowned. "Why? The food hasn't even arrived."

"If you want to get beaten up by my brothers, you better do as I say."

Drake raised an eyebrow and—of course—paid no heed to my warnings and turned around. Typical.

"Who told them we're here?" he grumbles, and I muttered under my breath while thinking of ways to get back at my interfering brothers.

"I don't even need three guesses to know."

Drake swore, and we sneaked out of the restaurant when my brothers weren't looking. We rushed into the car and drove off randomly.

"So, where do you want to go now since, I think, it's too late to get reservations at any restaurant?" Drake asked unhappily.

I shrugged, and my eyes widened as we passed by a McDonald's. "Wait, stop! Let's eat there!"

Drake shot me a bewildered look. "Really? You're serious?"

I nodded eagerly, my stomach rumbling with hunger. "Yeah. Hurry, I'm starving."

Drake grumbled. "You're really making it hard to impress you. McDonald's, seriously?"

I rolled my eyes and responded, "Yes. If you bring me there, I'll have no problem with being impressed with you."

So, there we sat in McDonald's, and I was munching happily on a cheeseburger, fries, and nuggets with a coke. Drake watched me intently with an occasional frown marring his face.

"What is it?"

Drake shot me an amused look. "Nothing. It's just that you eat a lot more than other girls."

I rolled my eyes and snapped defensively. "Well, I like food."

"Relax, sweetheart. I'm not saying anything. In fact, I like my woman more lush with curves."

My heart started beating faster, and I tried to hide the smile blooming on my face. Drake shot me a devilish grin and ran his fingers through his hair.

"Ready to go? It's too late to go where I wanted to take you, so I guess I have to send you back home."

Strangely, I felt disappointed. I mean, so far this date was fun, and I enjoyed myself with Drake although my brothers ruined a part of it.

"Oh, okay. What's your favorite color?" I suddenly blurted out, not wanting to end this date

Drake raised his eyebrows. "Green. Are you playing twenty questions with me?"

"Yeah. I just realized I know practically nothing about you."

"How cliché. Have you had sex before?" Drake grinned.

I spluttered. "You're supposed to ask me a decent question you're curious about!"

"I *am* curious if you ever had sex before." Drake grinned innocently.

"Yes, I have. Favorite sport besides racing?"

"Football. Ever had sex in public?"

"No! What's with all the sexual questions?" I said, a tad bit embarrassed.

Drake let a slow sensual smirk cross his face, and I could feel my heart beating faster. I almost wanted to give in and let Drake have his way with me.

I bit my lip and my eyes locked with Drake, and I could literally feel the temperature and atmosphere seem to rise in McDonald's.

"Let's get out of here," Drake said huskily.

I nodded and followed Drake to his car. My eyes wandered lustfully to Drake's arms, making his tattoo stand out even more.

"Your place or mine?" Drake all but growled as I placed my hand on his thigh.

"Yours. Unless you want to get interrupted."

When we reached the lobby of the building, Drake's shirt was already partially unbuttoned. In the lift, he had unzipped and unbuttoned my jeans. By the time we arrived at his apartment, Drake was no longer wearing his shirt. My knitted wear was partially off my body.

And I have to admit, as we made our way into Drake's room, occasionally bumping into walls or furniture, I could feel it was going to be the best night of my life.

CHAPTER 12-THE

MORNING

Olivia

I opened my eyes as I felt a hand trace my spine. I shifted to see Drake staring at me with a grin. "What are you looking at?"

Drake rested his head in his hands, making his biceps bulge, which resulted in me drooling inwardly. "Just liking how good you look in my bed, especially naked."

I bit back a blush when Drake raked his eyes all over me lustfully, but I had morals to follow. I was not going to be a booty call, friends with benefits, nor a one-night stand. No matter how good the sex was.

And of course, I knew I had to leave because Drake obviously doesn't do relationships. So, I left the bed and started dressing.

Drake got up and frowned. "Where are you going?"

I shrugged and said, "I know when I have to leave. You don't do relationships, so I get it."

I slipped on my shirt and opened the door to have it slammed shut before I could leave.

"What are you talking about?" Drake demanded as he stood over me nude. My eyes kept straying to Drake's muscled chest.

"You don't do relationships, and we had sex last night. I refuse to be a booty call whenever you need a fuck. So, I'm leaving so we can still be friends or whatever we are," I stated plainly.

"What if I don't want to just be friends with you?" Drake said quietly, his blue eyes burning into mine. "What if I finally found someone I don't mind being in a relationship with?"

My mouth opened and closed for a few moments. "What do you mean?"

Drake exhaled wearily. "I'm saying that I wouldn't mind having a relationship if it's with you. And no, not because of the sex, even though it was amazing, but because you intrigue me. You make me laugh, you surprise me, you fascinate me, and I like you as a person."

Whoa.

I was rendered speechless. Never in a million ways would I ever imagine Drake saying those words to a woman, especially me! I mean, he is a womanizer! No normal womanizer would say that. They would say a random pickup line and *bam*! The girl falls into the trap.

"So, what are you trying to say?" I questioned, squishing all traces of hope in my heart. For all I know, he may be talking about someone else entirely. Drake raised his eyebrows, and a small grin etched onto his face.

"I'm saying, I would like to be in a relationship with you. And if you don't get what I'm implying, I'm asking you if you would like to be my girlfriend, which is a highly coveted position most girls would like to be in."

"Drake, that's not helping."

"So, would you be my girlfriend?" Drake ignored me and demanded as he pressed his naked body against mine. His erection was pressed against me, and I could feel it throbbing against my stomach. I was stunned. I had an attraction for Drake, and I think I even liked him, pervert or not. But, never would I have imagined that my feelings would be reciprocated.

"What would I gain from being your girlfriend?" I asked, a hint of a smile on my lips.

Drake smirked. "Amazing, mindblowing sex, make out sessions, and being able to touch me…"

I raised an eyebrow, and said coyly, "That sounds good, but I'm not sure that'll be enough…" I trailed off.

"Oh, I forgot, being my girlfriend means that we can have shower sex." Drake grinned.

"I'm not quite sure what that means."

Drake grinned wickedly. "How about I demonstrate?" He picked me up and carried me to the bathroom.

"Wow, I didn't know you could cook," I said astounded as I watched Drake chop some onions quickly like a professional chef. Drake smiled as he tossed the diced onions into a boiling pot.

"My mother made sure I knew how to cook and clean for myself. Can you cook?"

I snorted. "No. I got my dad's gene of not being able to cook anything. He was able to burn anything in the kitchen even with a pancake maker. So, if you really like your house, never let me cook in here."

Drake laughed and ran his fingers through his wet hair.

"What are you making for me, anyway?"

"Pasta. I couldn't make an extravagant meal on such short notice," Drake answered as he frowned at the refrigerator. My eyes ran down the length of his body, and I licked my lips unconsciously. "Sweetheart, if you keep staring at me like that, we'll have another kind of meal."

Drake smirked and set a plate of pasta in front of me before sitting opposite me. "So, you have not said yes, yet."

I blinked before nodding. "Yeah. I'll be your girlfriend."

A smile formed on Drake's face as he stood up. "We can have lunch after we consummate this relationship." He picked me up as I laughed and we headed to his bedroom.

"Are we gonna stay here all day or are we heading back to your house?" Drake asked as he leisurely traced random patterns on my thighs. I froze.

Shit. Oh, my god!

I turned to Drake, who shot me a questioning glance.

"What? What's wrong?"

"My family! My dad and my brothers are going to kill you! What are you gonna do?"

Drake frowned and shrugged. "So what?" He stretched out on the bed and smirked. "I can *do* you… again."

I choked, and my face burned. "Drake! Be serious!" Right at that moment, my phone rang. I scrambled out of Drake's hold with the bed covers to get my phone from under my clothes.

"You do know I've seen everything right?"

I grimaced at Drake to see him lying proudly on the bed with an erection jutting out. I squeaked and immediately turned around.

"You're such a sex addict!" I turned around to grab my phone.

"Hello?"

"Honey? Where did you go? Tristan said you're with Drake. Your father and your brothers are not very... happy." My mother's quite concerned voice rang out.

I jumped when warm hands grabbed my hips. Drake nipped the shell of my ear before placing warm kisses down my neck. I bit back a moan and clutched the sheets to my body tighter.

"Honey? Livvy?"

I woke to my senses and pushed Drake away. "Uh, yeah. I'm at Drake's house." I shrieked as I felt the sheet being pulled away from me.

"Oh. Livvy, I trust you to know what you're doing, okay? Don't get yourself hurt."

I glared at Drake, who was raking his eyes over my body and slipped on my clothes from the floor as quickly as I could with one hand.

"Yeah. I know. I'm heading home soon." I bit my lip and sighed.

"Okay, then. Bye, honey."

All of a sudden, a hand grabbed me, and Drake pulled me against him. Even though I was clothed, I could still feel the warmth of his body.

Pushing my lustful thoughts away, I shifted away from him and ran my hands through my hair, inwardly wincing at how knotty it became.

"Drake, I need you to drop me home. My mom is worried about me."

I turned around, and Drake was leaning on the doorframe, clothed with a lustful glint in his eyes.

"What?" I snapped, trying not to blush.

"Nothing." Drake gave me a sensual grin and walked off.

Jeez, that man was a confusing piece of shit.

"Honey, be careful of your father. He's on a warpath today with your brothers," my mom said casually as she sipped her glass of iced tea.

My face blanched, and I scowled. "But who the hell told dad and your sons about Drake and me?!"

"Language!" my mom replied sharply before shrugging. "I don't really know. All I know is that Nate barged into our room without knocking when your dad was in the mood—"

"Mom! I don't want to hear about you and dad's sex life!" I moaned into my pillow while my mom shot me a wicked grin.

"I'll have you know that my sex life with your dad is what brought you here." My mom raised her eyebrows and rolled her eyes at my behavior. "And the next thing, Gabriel just stormed out with his jaw clenched."

I groaned in dismay and scowled at my mom. "Why didn't you distract him or something?"

"It's better sooner than later, right? Where's Drake, anyway? He better not get you pregnant unless I see a ring on that finger."

"Mom!" I blushed furiously. It was extremely awful and embarrassing to talk about this sort of things with my mom.

"No one's getting you pregnant or getting you married unless I say so! You hear me?" My father crossed his arms, his massive frame covering almost the entire doorframe. His eyes bore into mine with determination.

Oh hell.

CHAPTER 13-THE RULES

Olivia

"Repeat the rules," my father demanded.

"I must stay a meter away from Drake. I cannot hold his hand. I am not allowed to share body fluids with him. I am not allowed to be alone with him. I will not share the same bed as Drake. I must be properly dressed around him at all times. Is that all, sir?" I finished mockingly.

My father folded his arms and ignored my comment. "If you don't follow, you're grounded until you're thirty."

My eyes widened, and I gaped at him shocked. "Are you insane? I'm twenty-three not sixteen. I'm a fully grown adult, and you can't treat me like I'm not."

"Gabriel, that's not sensible. Those rules are ridiculous. They're a couple, and they can't hold hands? We held hands and broke all your golden rules before we got married." My mom frowned at my dad as she pointed that bit out.

My dad spluttered and turned a bit red. "Well, it's different. She's my daughter."

"She's *my* daughter, too. Olivia is an adult, and we will treat her as such! Is that clear?" My mom crossed her arms and shot back.

My dad was about to retort when my mom glared at him. "Fine. Whatever." With that, my dad stalked out of the room, leaving my mom and me in the empty study.

"How could you have married someone like that?" I burst out, and my mom gracefully sat down and laughed.

"Honey, your father is just looking out for you. Nothing else. You're his princess, and he just can't accept the fact that all his daughters are leading their own lives." My mom smiled at me, and I instantly felt guilty.

I sighed. "I know. It's just that he gets carried away and becomes overbearing, and it doesn't help that your sons are helping him." I shot a dirty look at my mom.

She laughed. "Well, they're your brothers."

"You should've name all three of them 'Gabriel,'" I muttered, and my mom laughed.

"Now, that would be fun, wouldn't it?"

I scowled, trying to hold back a smile but failed.

The knocking on the door interrupted my retort as Phillip toddled his way to me. "Livvy!"

"Hey, Phillip! Where's mommy?" I bent down and picked him up.

"Oh, Liv, honey, your brothers have gone to Canada to watch an ice-hockey game, and they won't be back until next week."

My head snapped up at that piece of information. "Oh really?" I asked, trying not to let my excitement show. Crazy as it was, I longed to be near Drake again.

"Really," my mom said knowingly.

I bit my lip to hold back a grin and helped Phillip back to his room.

I guess it must be some kind of coincidence that Drake called me at that exact moment, asking if he wanted me to see him racing in two hours.

The minute I arrived, I forgot one thing. There were paparazzi everywhere.

Shit.

I had completely forgotten that in racing events like this, there would be news reporters around. I gritted my teeth as suddenly, all the attention was on me. I was so going to kill Drake.

Even though I was born famous, I didn't particularly enjoy the attention. I didn't like my personal information being splashed across websites or gossip magazines.

A bunch of people started flashing their cameras and asking me questions. Drake tried his best to make way for me, but there were too many people blocking our path.

"Olivia! Why are you here at a race?"

"Olivia! Are you meeting anyone here?"

"Do you have a boyfriend who is a racer?"

I forced a smile on my face and ignored them until an arm was wrapped around my shoulder and spoke, "Yeah, it's me."

Immediately, there were flashes, and questions were being shouted. I glared at Drake, only for it to fade when I realized he was wearing a skin-tight white v-neck shirt with his racing jumpsuit worn only at his hips. The white shirt emphasized his muscles and abs, and I was ashamed to say that I forgot that we were in a crowd.

A smirk formed on his face, and I snapped myself out of it. I forced another smile on my face and smiled at the cameras.

"How long have you been together?"

"How did you two meet?"

Drake smirked down at me and shrugged casually as his arm dropped from my shoulders and wrapped around my waist tightly. "Well, I'll let you know later. After all, Olivia came to see me win this year again."

With that, he pulled me along with him past the crowd and into the arena. He smirked down at me, his eyes lingering on the bust of my dress. I slapped his arm, and he looked at me charmingly.

"What?"

"You're such a pervert."

"It's not my fault you're so hot."

I flushed. "Drake!"

"Okay, okay. Come, let's go. There's a private seating for special guests of the racers. I have to go get ready. What about a kiss for good luck?"

I shot him a flat look, and Drake grinned. "It was worth a shot." I scowled at him and sat next to a pregnant blonde.

"Hi, I'm Lena. Who are you here for?"

I blinked. "Oh, I'm here for my boyfriend, Drake. I'm Olivia Ford."

Lena grinned at me. "Drake is your boyfriend? Wow, never thought he'll get one with all those women around him all the time."

My smile froze, and I stiffened. I knew Drake had been with other girls before because he was a womanizer, but it still wasn't any easier hearing about it. Uncomfortable about the topic, I bent down slightly and played with the skirt of my dress before giving her a tight smile.

"Oh! Forget what I said. Rick did say that Drake was all moony about some blonde girl for weeks, but he never said who." Lena smiled at me.

I frowned in confusion. "I'm sorry, who's Rick?"

Lena laughed. "Oh, I'm sorry! Rick is my husband and Drake's manager. Drake is like another annoying brother to me."

I nodded, not knowing what to say. "So is the baby a he or she?" I gestured towards her big belly.

Lena grinned and patted the bump. "A girl. Finally, after two boys. At first, I was really angry at Rick that he got me pregnant again after our two boys, but when I found out it was a girl, I was so excited!"

I beamed, feeling excited with her.

"So, Olivia, how did you meet Drake?"

I shrugged and shook my head. "I work as a part-time air stewardess, and Drake asked me to have a quickie with him in the washroom, and I told him no."

Lena gasped and looked at me with recognition in her eyes. "So, you're the one that Drake kept complaining about."

"What did he say about me?"

A wicked gleam entered Lena's eyes, and she laughed. "He said that how could anyone resist him and that he was Drake Henderson and you ought to be begging to have sex with him. Of course, when I heard that, I slapped him on the head."

My jaw dropped, and I scoffed before rolling my eyes. One day, Drake's arrogance was going to be the death of himself.

"Oh, dear god," I mumbled and shook my head.

"I know! By the way, is your brother, uh, ah... Nathaniel, still single?"

I choked and turned to her with wide eyes. "Um, what?"

"He is really hot, and after he had gone to the army, he got really muscled. Rick works out and has some muscles but not as nice as your brother's," Lena said, grinning.

I laughed and snorted as I imagined Nate cringing at the very pregnant Lena chasing after him. It was clear that

Lena was joking, the love she had for Rick was clear as day.

"Oh, look, the race is starting. There, the black car with red and white stripes, that's Drake's car."

I watched as the spectators in the arena grew more excited as the horn flared. Immediately, the cars zoomed off with astonishing speed. I spotted Drake driving the car with ease and weaving in and out of the way of other cars. A blue car followed his, and I watched in horror as the car tried to slam into his car.

"Lena, who's driving the blue car?"

"Hmm? Oh, that's Drew Wilson. He's always getting first runner-up after Drake, and he's pretty resentful about it all these years."

I frowned. Drew Wilson was a very familiar name that I couldn't remember where I've heard it before. Drew Wilson. *Wilson. Ugh, I still couldn't remember it.*

"Where did he come from?" I asked curiously.

Lena shrugged and chewed on a biscuit as she answered, "He's from England and studying at Yale, but he took over his father in racing a few years ago."

"Oh." I couldn't help but watch in worry as the blue car attempted to knock Drake into the fence again. "Isn't he playing dirty?" I asked worriedly.

"Yeah, but he doesn't care. Don't worry, Drake always manages to avoid Drew."

I watched in anticipation as the race went on and cheered as Drake neared the finish line and crossed it. I let out a sigh of relief, and my shoulders visibly sagged.

"He's good, isn't he?"

I nodded. "Yeah."

"Come! Let's go down to congratulate him. I can introduce you to my husband and two sons!" Lena squealed excitedly as she waddled along due to her very pregnant belly.

I followed her and gaped at the huge crowd swarming the entire arena.

I spotted Drake with a huge trophy in his hands, a group of reporters surrounding him. Trying to avoid the attention, I turned away until Drake yelled my name out and went towards me. The huge crowd of reporters followed after him eagerly when they spotted me as well. I stiffened as he came up to me. Forcing another tight smile on my face, I avoided looking at the cameras but focused on him.

"Aren't you gonna give me a congratulatory kiss?" I flushed and leaned in to give him a small peck on the cheek. I guessed Drake saw that coming as he turned his head to meet mine. I froze until Drake wrapped an arm around my waist and his other hand cradled my cheek. Immediately, I melted and kissed him back.

His tongue delved into my mouth and his arms wrapped around my waist tightly. I pulled away dazedly while Drake smirked down at me.

"Drake! How long have you been together?"

"Olivia! Are both of you getting married?"

Drake grabbed my waist and gave the paparazzi a heartbreaking grin. "Maybe. It's too soon to tell. Good day, folks." He grabbed my hand and pulled me away to the private seating.

"Sweetheart, meet Rick. He's my ass of a manager, by the way. Rick, meet Olivia Ford. My girlfriend." Drake introduced me to a middle-aged man with two boys in his arms. Lena was standing beside him happily. Rick rolled his eyes at Drake's comment before giving me a grin.

"Hi, I'm really sorry about Drake. He has no manners," I said apologetically, and Drake snorted. I shot him a glare and Rick laughed.

"It's nice to meet you, Olivia. I can see that you're keeping Drake in line. Great job, by the way."

I laughed as Drake smirked. "I'm only listening to her because of the se—"

"Henderson! Shut it!" I hissed as I slapped a hand over his mouth. I was totally mortified. He had some nerve for spilling private information in public! Drake laughed, and I punched him in the arm.

"I'm kidding, sweetheart." He gave me a smug grin.

I bit my lip and tried to resist smacking him once more, and my eyes met Rick's amused ones.

I blushed, and one of Rick's sons gurgled happily and tugged on his hair painfully. "Ow, Max! That hurts!" Rick winced in pain, and Lena laughed before taking Max into her arms. Drake sighed beside me and stiffened as a figure made his way towards us.

"Well, look, here's the champion again, Drake Henderson," a cocky, cold, arrogant voice called out. I watched Drake put on a cool facade and turned around.

The man walking towards us had the same height as Drake. He had blond hair and ice-blue eyes that were filled with arrogance and a hint of resentment. He also had a strong jaw. I would have found him cute had it been his demeanor was the opposite of cold.

"Congratulations again this year, Henderson."

Drake shrugged nonchalantly. "It was another easy feat, considering you tried to get me into an accident, Wilson, but I managed again."

The man in front of us clenched his jaw, and his fists tightened as the atmosphere rose with thick heavy tension.

"Well, I guess I have to try harder again next year. Who's your pretty friend?" His ice-cold eyes glanced at me, and I held back the shudder of unease that went through me.

"I'm Olivia Ford."

His eyes flickered with recognition. "I'm Drew Wilson. Your grandmother Leslie should have introduced us by now, but she had claimed that you were already... taken."

Right! Drew was the boy that my nanny Leslie had wanted me to meet back at Ellie's engagement ball. I noticed Drake's hand around my hip was getting tighter as Drew spoke.

I shrugged. "Yes, I'm sorry, but she was right. I am taken," I said awkwardly, and I could tell that Drake was smirking smugly as his hand gripped my waist possessively.

Drew frowned and shrugged nonchalantly. "Well, I guess when you're bored with Henderson, you could give me a call. My grandmother approves of you."

What was wrong with this guy? Wasn't it obvious that I wasn't interested? Or was he purposely trying to goad Drake?

"Okay, Wilson, you can leave *now*. She's with me," Drake said evenly.

I glanced up at Drake in surprise. His jaw was clenched, and his eyes were glaring into Drew. I had never heard him use such a cold tone before.

"I'll see you later, Olivia." With that, Drew walked off.

I frowned. Drew didn't give me a good feeling.

CHAPTER 14-THE LOVE CONFESSION

Olivia

"I love you."

I blinked, the three words not fully processed in my mind. "Excuse me?"

"I love you, Olivia, ever since we were kids."

"But... I... you... Um. How? Why? Wait. What?" I stammered, shocked by his declaration.

Vincent chuckled and smiled at me. He took my hand in his and smiled. "I... Love... You," he repeated slowly.

Seven hours ago.

I bit my lip as I scanned the web page rapidly. It seemed like Drake and I dating was hot news even though it had been a month since my appearance at his race.

Okay, maybe I was just curious what the public had to say about Drake and I dating. And because of that, I was now googling for articles online.

Heiress and the racer?
Playboy gets a rich catch?
Henderson talks marriage with Ford!

Wait, what? Marriage? What! I clicked on the link, and the page showed.

When asked if hot heiress Olivia Ford is his girlfriend, Drake Henderson had said yes immediately with a possessive arm around her waist. Who knew that playboy Henderson could be so possessive when he had girls lining up to get a piece of him? Drake and Olivia are one of the hottest couples around especially when no one had anticipated this match! Let's also not forget the hot make-out session when Drake had been awarded the championship title! When questioned about marriage, Drake had merely said, "Maybe. It's too soon to tell." Well, it wasn't an outright no! Hopefully, wedding bells would be sounded especially when Olivia Ford is playboy Drake's first and hopefully last girlfriend! This author has her fingers crossed that their love story of a girl changing a womanizer's ways would indeed come true!

What... On... Earth... Is... This? I was his first girlfriend? That made me feel quite flattered. I started grinning idiotically to myself until what the main topic of the article was about.

Marriage... With... Drake.

Somehow, I could picture myself getting married to him, but who was I kidding? Drake wasn't one for long-term relationships. I guess we would only be together until either one of us was tired of each other.

Even though we were together for about a month, I thought I'll eventually get bored with Drake, but somehow, I seemed to crave his presence. It was frightening and yet exhilarating.

I frowned and glanced at my phone, Drake hadn't called today at all. I didn't want to seem like a clingy girlfriend, but I missed him. It was weird feeling this way. Even though Drake was full of sexual innuendos or jokes, he could be incredibly sweet at times, not that I was going to tell him that. I didn't want his ego getting more inflated.

I glanced at my phone again and hastily put it down. I was *not* going to be annoying and clingy.

"What's this?" an angry voice sounded out behind me.

I jumped up in fright and realized that it was Jacob, one of my siblings.

I rolled my eyes and turned around in my swivel chair. "Jake! Get out of my room," I yelled, and I tried to push him out.

"Not until you tell me what's going on!" Jake snapped as he tossed me a gossip magazine with Drake and me on the cover with our lips locked. I flushed and tried to cover my blush with a glare.

"Drake and I dating is none of your business!" I said annoyed. I folded my arms and glared at him.

He gritted his teeth. "It is because you're my little sister!"

"And you're my older brother who slept with my best friend in senior year!"

I watched in satisfaction as my brother paled before blinking.

"W-what? Wait. How did you know?"

I rolled my eyes. "I think I would know when she yelled at me and told me she refused to be friends with a girl whose brother is a fucking whore."

Jake's mouth opened and closed for a while before looking sheepish. "Well, now, at least thanks to me you know she isn't such a good friend? And, if you knew about it long ago, why didn't you confront me about it?"

I smirked. "To save it for moments like these. If you do anything to Drake or me or try to ruin our relationship, I'll tell mom. We all know how much she loved Zoe like another daughter. And when she learns that you took her virginity and made her leave, I wonder what she'll say because basically, shit will hit the fan."

Jake narrowed his eyes. "Are you blackmailing me?"

I knew he had given in. His shoulders slackened, and his nostrils flared in annoyance. "Fine. She was a lousy lay, anyway." He stalked out of the room.

I grinned in triumph and smirked to myself smugly. It wasn't often I got one over my brothers, and I relished in it.

"Livvy! Let's go for dress fittings!" Ellie came into my room, beaming.

I frowned, confused. "I thought I didn't need to anymore?"

Ellie blushed and looked away sheepishly. "Um, the red dress was not your bridesmaid dress. It was for fun, considering Drake was there."

My jaw dropped. "Elena Sophia Ford, how could you? I felt so awful in that red dress!"

Ellie giggled. "At least you could pull it off and look hot. It was funny to see Drake looking at you like he wanted to eat you!"

I glared at her, and her giggles subsided. "Okay, okay, I'm sorry. But I really, really wanted you and Drake to be together. You guys look great as a couple. And I've come to bring you to the actual dress fitting," Ellie said happily.

I sighed. Ellie had her quirks for being a matchmaker. "Okay, let's go."

Ellie beamed happily before walking off.

I slipped on the baby blue dress and opened the curtains of the dressing room. Immediately, gasps sounded off, and I fidgeted, not liking the sudden attention.

"Wow. Olivia, you look amazing!" Lily gushed with a sulky-looking Phillip to her right and a sleeping Penny on her lap.

Ellie clapped her hands excitedly. "I knew that dress would fit you! You look like a princess!"

I smiled awkwardly. "Shouldn't you be the one looking like the princess on *your* wedding day?" I said.

Ellie grinned happily. "I know, but you are wearing that. I don't care how many protests you have in your head, but you are going to wear that dress!"

I sighed. Ellie was as stubborn as stubborn gets. There was no way I could argue my way out of this. I turned to look in the mirror, and a small smile graced my lips. The dress had a heart-shaped neckline, and the sleeves were all made with lace. At the waistline, it was figure-hugging until it flowed out in an A-line skirt to my knees. It had white beading on it with amazing floral designs. It was beautiful, and I was in love with it.

"Okay, I'll wear it." I gave in and watched Ellie clap her hands in excitement.

"Great!"

Ellie stepped away, and I drew the curtains shut.

As I slipped on my dress, my phone rang. The minute I saw his name, my heart started beating faster. "Hello?"

"Hey, Liv! I'm bringing you out for lunch. Meet you outside that new restaurant that just opened the other day!" With that, Drake just hung up. I blinked and rolled my eyes, putting down the phone.

I walked out of the bridal shop after saying my goodbyes and started making my way to the restaurant when Vincent caught up with me.

"Hey, Olive!" Vincent smiled at me, and immediately, I smiled back. But thoughts of what Vincent might feel for me rose in my head.

"Wanna head for lunch?"

I bit my lip. "I'm meeting Drake for lunch nearby."

Vincent's eyes hardened slightly, and he shrugged casually. "I'll wait until he comes."

I pursed my lips and nodded. "Okay. That'll be great."

We made small talk, and once we were seated, Vincent grinned charmingly at me.

"Livvy, I'm in love with this one girl."

I gasped and bit my lip, hoping that this turn of conversation would not be heading to where I think it is going. "Oh, who is this girl?" I asked lamely.

"You, Olivia," Vincent said out loud. His eyes never left my face. "I love you," he continued.

I blinked, the three words not fully processed in my mind. "Excuse me?" I stammered and watched him with wide eyes. Sure, I've suspected his feelings for me, but I never imagined that he would confess it.

"I love you, Olivia, ever since we were kids."

"But… I… you… um. How? Why? Wait. What?" I stammered, shocked by his declaration. Vincent chuckled and smiled at me.

He took my hand in his and smiled. "I… Love… You," he repeated slowly

"I… I… I…" I stammered stupidly, and my brain shut down. I had no idea what to say! *Oh gosh! What do I say? Word vomit would have been nice as well.*

"Get the fuck out of my seat! Get away from my girl and get the hell out of here!"

I looked up and saw a pissed off Drake shooting daggers with his eyes at Vincent, who would probably be dead by now if those were real. And if I remember correctly, Vincent did not bow down to anyone. He stood up and faced Drake with a threatening glare.

Shit just basically hit the fan.

CHAPTER 15-THE HARSH WORDS

Olivia

"I said, step the fuck away from her," Drake said quietly, his eyes hard and his jaw clenched.

Vincent shifted his jaw and stared at him defiantly, his eyes flashing. "What if I don't want to? You don't even deserve her."

Drake tensed before grabbing my hand and pulled me out of the restaurant. I was thankful for that for we were attracting the attention of almost every person in that restaurant.

We were outside the restaurant and walking away when Vincent grabbed my other hand.

Drake and I were jerked to a stop, and I was pulled towards Drake. "Get your bloody hands off her, you prick."

Vincent clutched my hand tighter and pulled me towards him. "Like I said before, you don't deserve her. You don't even deserve to breathe the same air as her!"

Oh, I can see where this is going. All three of us will be playing tug of war. I'll be the bloody piece of rope!

Drake narrowed his eyes, letting go of my hands completely before pulling me abruptly to his side. I stumbled a little before righting myself and dreaded the violent confrontation that was starting to brew right in front of me.

Vincent's jaw clenched, and without warning, he swung a fist in Drake's direction. Drake ducked, and his fist collided with Vincent's face. I cringed at the sight of blood gushing out of Vincent's nose. Vincent let out a cry of pain, and I gasped.

"Drake, stop it. You made your point!"

I tried tugging him away, but he was way too strong.

"You had better stay away from her, Forrer. She chose me over you. Deal with it," Drake said as he clenched his jaw. With that, Drake stalked off as he grabbed my hand with him.

I bit my lip as Drake got into his car and I entered hesitantly. "Drake."

"What he said was true, wasn't it?" Drake said forcefully.

"Huh?" I asked stupidly. Pretty sure I looked like a gaping goldfish at the moment.

His fingers clenched around the steering wheel until his knuckles turned white. "About me not deserving you."

I blinked. "I—"

"I'm sorry." He interrupted me.

My jaw dropped. He wasn't going to break up with me, was he? I bit my lip as he continued, "Vincent is right. I don't deserve you, but I'm sorry. I'm too much of a selfish asshole to let you go. You're the only good thing that's going on for me now in my life."

My heart fluttered, and I blushed, and a goofy grin appeared on my face. Drake glanced at me, and a smirk tugged onto the corner of his lips before glancing back at the road.

Did that mean Drake still wanted me around? Drake interlaced our fingers and held on tightly as he drove with his left hand.

I bit my lip before a cheesy smile can escape on my face. My smile faded when what really happened sank in. Drake hit one of my best friends. I felt sorry for Vincent. Getting rejected and hit for trying made me feel guilty.

Drake and I had to apologize. After all, he was still my best friend.

"Drake?" I said hesitantly.

"Yeah, sweetheart?" Drake replied as he gave me a quick glance before turning his attention to the road.

"We have to apologize to Vincent."

"What? Why the fuck should I? He's trying to take what is mine! And I don't share!" Drake said coldly.

I frowned, not liking to be treated as a possession. "Drake, I'm not a toy you two should fight about. We should apologize. We embarrassed him in public, me rejecting him and you hitting him."

"I do not apologize to people."

"You ought to! At least to him. No matter what he did, he was my best friend," I said, watching him warily.

"Stop telling me what to do! I do as I please. If I don't want to apologize to him, I would not!" Drake said, his voice now louder.

"But that's the right thing to do—"

"For fuck's sake, would you stop being such a controlling bitch?" he yelled as his hand slammed against the dashboard, and I froze.

His words stabbed me in my heart, and I could feel my stomach falling. My eyes welled up with tears.

"Olivia, I—" Drake realized what he said and turned towards me with regret in his eyes.

"Oh. I didn't know that's how you feel about me," I said quietly.

His words rang in my ears, and I held back my tears. It felt like someone had punched me in the gut. I had to go. I didn't want to be in Drake's presence. Conveniently, the car had stopped as the traffic lights turned red.

"Olivia, I… I didn't mean—"

I hurriedly unsnapped the safety belt before getting out of the car.

As I got out, I rushed off as the tears started to fall, leaving Drake shouting my name.

CHAPTER 16-THE MAKING UP

Olivia

I sniffled into my pillow as my grandmother Leslie sat next to me on the bed.

"I'm sure he didn't mean it, dear. All you had is a little spat. He never had a girlfriend before, so I'm sure he has a bit of trouble figuring how to make a relationship work. Relationships are all about compromise. You give in a bit to each other."

I sniffled again. "But I'm sure he meant it, or else he wouldn't have said it. I'm not controlling, am I?"

It has been two days since the incident, and I've been crying my eyes out. I guess Drake and I were no longer dating, or we were on a break. My heart ached from his absence and his hurtful words.

"No, of course, he didn't. Words from anger are never meant. Besides, both of you are meant for each other. You're just having a little fight. Come, I have a little surprise to cheer you up that can fix this little issue." My grandmother grinned at me, a sly glint in her eyes.

Was I ready to make up with Drake?

No. Even though I missed him, his words cut deep, and they hurt. Oh, they hurt. It brought up all my insecurities of being unworthy to be loved and wanting me just for my money.

"Come, dear." My grandmother led me to the lounge where another elderly lady was with a man. I frowned, the man was not Drake. I could not see his face for his back was facing me.

"Leslie!" the elderly lady greeted, and the man stood to face us. I paled. He was Drew Wilson, and the other woman was probably his grandmother, Henrietta.

Was this a matchmaking plan? Good God, I was in no way mentally or emotionally prepared to deal with this. However, my grandmother had said this would fix my problem with Drake, which it definitely wouldn't. What on earth was my grandmother doing?

"Hello, Henrietta! You must be Drew. You certainly take after your father. Come, come, and meet my granddaughter, Olivia."

Drew watched me intently with scrutinizing eyes before taking my hand to place a kiss and said smoothly, "We already met, Leslie. I told you, you'll be seeing me again soon."

I nodded my head uncomfortably. Somehow, Drew gave me the creeps. "Oh, yes. Hello, Mrs. Wilson and Drew."

Henrietta grinned at me. "I approve of her, Drew. Call me Henrietta."

I flushed from discomfort at the older woman's statement and glanced at my grandmother who ushered Drew to sit beside me.

"So, you're single now? Leslie said so. Guess Henderson found someone else."

My grandmother and Henrietta had left the lounge and had gone somewhere else.

I bit my lip. Drew's words brought another question to my mind. Had Drake been with someone else for these past two days? My heart clenched, and I forced a smile onto my face.

"Oh. Actually, um, we just had a fight," I stated tonelessly and fidgeted under Drew's narrowed eyes that had turned cold.

"Is that so? I saw him the day before yesterday fucking a blonde," he said coldly, and my heart fell to the bottom of my stomach.

Could it be? I didn't know what to believe. Could Drake have really done that? Yes. He could. He used to be a playboy, wasn't he? Yet, I knew I couldn't simply trust Drew. He hated Drake, and I had to have faith in him. But it was hard to, simply hearing those words from Drew or anyone felt like someone daggered me in the heart.

"I don't believe you," I said quietly.

Drew simply raised an eyebrow before continuing, "Did I also mention that the blonde looked quite like you? I guess he found a replacement. Be with me, and you could get back at him. It would kill him to know that you are with me, his rival."

Again, his words slapped me so hard, but I remained strong. However, I was curious to know what had happened between Drake and Drew.

"Fuck off, Wilson," a voice said coldly before hands grabbed my waist, and I was hefted over a shoulder. I blinked and realized my face was facing Drake's back.

I struggled, Drake hit my bottom, and I gasped. He shifted me and my nose pressed against his back. I inhaled his shirt, searching for the smell of cologne, musk, and sandalwood which was Drake. What I got was cigarette smoke. I recoiled in horror, and Drake put me down in my room.

"You smoke?" I asked quietly.

"Used to," Drake replied.

My heart leaped in my chest just because of Drake's presence, but I wasn't ready to forgive him just yet. My eyes drank Drake in greedily, his hair was unkempt and his clothes were wrinkled. He looked like he had not been taking care of himself for the past two days but he still looked ruggedly gorgeous.

We stood there staring at each other for quite a while before I spoke.

"What are you doing here, Drake?" I said, wanting to throw my arms around him just to have body contact.

"I wanted, no, I needed to see you," Drake said, his blue eyes meeting mine.

"Why?"

"I-I missed you."

My traitorous heart started jumping wildly. "Oh," I murmured, my eyes meeting his.

"Olivia, I—" He stopped and ran his fingers through his hair nervously. "Look. I-I'm not good with apologies. I've probably only apologized twice in my life. But, I'm apologizing to you. I'm sorry for what I said to you in the car. I was frustrated and angry with Vincent, and you also continued to push me to apologize to him and for what I said— I didn't mean it. I am sorry.

"And I never cheated on you. What Drew said was a lie."

I could see the truth in his eyes, and I nodded.

I knew it was extremely difficult for Drake to say sorry to anyone. And it meant a lot to me that he apologized. "Okay. I accept your apology."

With that, I hugged him tightly, feeling the tension coiled up in his body fade away.

Drake wrapped his arms around me tightly as he hugged me back. "God, I missed you." The next thing I knew, Drake's mouth was on mine, and his hands were roaming all over my body.

I sighed contentedly, my left hand and my head resting on Drake's chest. Drake was silent as his fingers drew lazy patterns on my bare back.

"I—" Drake said suddenly but stopped, and I turned towards him in question.

"I'm not good at talking about feelings. The only good thing I can do with females is sex. But I had never been in a relationship before, so I can't—"

I gave a small smile. "I understand. We can figure this relationship thing out together."

My grandmother was right. Drake didn't know much about being in a relationship, and he had trouble expressing himself. I could deal with that. Thank goodness most of my family members were not around seeing that Drake and I had a fight.

Drake seemed surprised by my response before giving me a satisfied grin and tugged me underneath him.

His erection pressed against my stomach, and I gaped at him. "Again? You can't be serious!"

He gave me a smirk. "For you, always." With that, he crashed his mouth against mine.

CHAPTER 17-THE MIX UP

Olivia

I watched in awe as Drake made breakfast. It has been about two weeks since the entire incident with Vincent. He had made peace about me being with Drake and had left to meet his father two days ago.

"Livvy, dear."

"Hmm?" I sighed into the phone as Drake glanced at me while he flipped a pancake.

"Oh, honey, do you remember your friend Adrianna Valdez?"

Adrianna was one of my good friends since I was young. However, she had lost her boyfriend and fiancé when she was seventeen. We were still in high school. She was devastated and sunk into severe depression. Immediately, her parents wanted her to fly back home to Spain. We've kept in contact, and I missed her a lot.

I sat up straight at the kitchen counter. "Yeah, of course! Why?"

"She would be visiting for a while. In fact, she will be landing in less than an hour. Andre will meet you there to make sure she arrives safely before going back to Spain."

"Andre is back from the army?" I said, astounded. Andre is Adrianna's older brother whom I had not seen in years.

At the mention of a male name, Drake turned around and glanced at me, his eyes narrowing.

"Alright, dear. Goodbye."

I sighed happily, putting the phone back on the counter.

"Who's Andre?"

I looked up to see Drake watching me intently.

"That was my mom, and I'm fetching one of my childhood friends, who is going to stay with us, in a while. Andre is the older brother of my friend Adrian-"

"An Adrian has to live with you?" Drake glared at me.

I rolled my eyes. "It's not like that! Adri-"

"Don't say his name! Let's go and meet him shall we?" With that, he walked out of the house.

I rolled my eyes. "It's not what you think." Honestly, he was such an idiot at times.

"I know where this is going! Why didn't you ever mention an Adrian before?" Drake demanded.

I snorted. "Will you just listen for a minute and maybe you won't be such an ass?"

Drake scowled at me. "I am not an ass!"

I rolled my eyes in annoyance. "It's not like that!" I snapped. I glared at him and stalked out of the house, annoyed. Drake trailed behind me and got into the car.

"What are you doing here?"

"Following you. Let's go meet this Adrian guy."

I rolled my eyes before driving off. Immediately, Drake's left hand landed on my thigh. I shot him a quick glance before ignoring him.

Soon, his hand started trailing along my leg. Desire started creeping on to me, and I shot him an annoyed look. "Knock it off."

Drake smirked at me before lacing his fingers with mine, his head facing straight.

Drake was still an enigma to me. Sometimes, I couldn't figure out what he was thinking or the thoughts behind his actions.

When we reached the airport, I craned my neck looking for Adrianna. We had kept in touch and sent photos of each other over the years.

My eyes brightened when I saw my tall friend looking around for me. A man followed behind helping her with her luggage. "Adrianna! Andre! Here!"

"*What?*" Drake sputtered.

Adrianna noticed me, and a smile formed on her face before making her way towards me.

"Hey Adri, Andre."

Andre simply nodded his head towards me in acknowledgment before leaving.

I hugged Adrianna tightly. It had been many years since I last saw her, in short, I missed her. I pulled back to look at her.

"Hello, Olivia."

"Aren't you supposed to be a guy?" Drake questioned with his arms crossed.

Adrianna looked at him like he lost his mind while I couldn't help but enjoy the confused expression on his face.

"Drake, this is one of my best friends, *Adrianna* Valdez. Adri, this is Drake, my boyfriend," I said smugly.

Drake turned bright red before excusing himself to the car.

"I didn't know you had a boyfriend." Adrianna grinned at me.

I blushed. "It was pretty sudden, actually. I'll tell you all about it later."

"What is with your boyfriend for asking me if I am a male?" Adrianna asked curiously as we walked towards the car.

"He was a jealous ass who thought I meant an Adrian, not Adrianna. Even though I told him, it wasn't what he thought."

Adrianna laughed as she fingered a ring on her necklace. My eyes drifted to it, and I hesitantly asked, "Is that…?"

Immediately, Adrianna stopped laughing before her gaze dropped to the ground. "Yes."

I bit my lip, I should not have asked. The ring Adrianna had was her engagement ring from her fiancé when she was seventeen. However, he died in a car accident a week later. That was six years ago.

"Hi, my name is Drake Henderson. Sorry for the awkward and rude introduction. You're Adrianna, not Adrian. It was a little misunderstanding between Olivia and me."

Adrianna smirked before grinning. "Okay then. I'm happy for you both as long as you make her happy. She means a lot to me."

I gave a nervous laugh before gesturing to the car. "Why don't we get a move on?"

Drake drove this time while I sat behind with Adrianna. "So Drake, how did you meet Olivia?"

I gave out a short laugh before Drake smirked at us through the mirror.

"Oh, that. Olivia was an air stewardess on the flight I was on. I thought she was pretty hot and asked her to have a quickie with me in the washrooms.

"It was a shock when she refused. It was the first time that it ever happened. After that, I was intrigued. It was maybe a few days after when I met her again at her home during her sister's engagement party."

Adrianna looked amused as she turned to me. "Which sister of yours is engaged?"

"Ellie. She's getting married to Drake's older brother, Scott."

Adrianna looked impressed. "Wow, your brother really has guts or really loves Ellie. She can be overly emotional all the time."

Drake laughed. "Scott loves her. I've seen Ellie when she was angry, and she switched to weepy in just five seconds. I thank my guardian angel that Olivia isn't like her because I have no idea how to handle people like that."

Adrianna laughed, and I felt elated that my best friend and boyfriend got along very well.

CHAPTER 18-THE PAST

Drake

I watched Olivia laughing along with her sisters while her nephew Phillip sat on my lap. A little smile graced my lips, and I couldn't help admire how gorgeous she looked.

God, when did I become such a pansy?

"I can see you make Olivia happy." Adrianna sat down elegantly opposite me.

It had just been yesterday that Adrianna had arrived from Spain. She smiled at me gently before observing me quietly.

"Yeah, but she makes me happy too," I replied not knowing what to say. I hardly knew her after all.

Adrianna beamed happily. "That is good. But if you break her heart, I will kill you."

I shrugged. "I know, but you don't have to worry. I won't do anything to hurt her."

"You are in love with her, aren't you?" Adrianna asked me, a grin on her face.

I frowned. "No, I'm not. I just really like her."

Adrianna watched me carefully. "Something is holding you back. I can see it in your eyes. What happened to you?"

I stiffened. "I have no idea what you're talking about. I just don't believe in love."

Adrianna cocked an eyebrow and shot me a disbelieving glance. "Right. And I bet whatever you have been through is something you have not told Olivia."

I narrowed my eyes, I didn't like being psychologically analyzed. I had a messed up childhood that I did not want to share with others.

"It is none of your business. I don't love anyone except for my family." I gritted my teeth as I crossed my arms and stared down at Adrianna defiantly.

She shrugged casually. "Would you do anything for her if she asked?"

What was this fucking crazy woman talking about? Doesn't she see how much I cared for Olivia?

"Of course, if it was to make her happy."

Adrianna continued, "Would you take a bullet for her? Or would you kill for her?"

I considered her words. If anyone had ever hurt Olivia emotionally or physically, I would kill them. And if

Olivia were ever in danger, I would take the bullet, she deserved to live more than I did.

"Yes, I would," I answered.

"One last question, if Olivia left you for someone else, would you let her go willingly because that would make her happy?"

I clenched my jaw, what was this woman going on about? The fact that Olivia could leave me to be with someone else?

No way in fucking hell.

"No, what the hell are you talking about? If she did, I would fight tooth and nail for her."

A small smile graced Adrianna's face. "You're in love with her, Drake."

I narrowed my eyes. "I said I am not! I just care for her. Love doesn't exist! It never has and it never will. What do you know about love, anyway?" I said coldly.

At this, Adrianna's gaze fell to the ground as she said quietly, "My fiancé died six years ago. I loved him very much. In fact, I still do."

Immediately, I felt guilty. "I'm sorry."

"He died in a car accident when we were seventeen." Adrianna continued as if she had not heard me. "I don't like to talk about him and his death." Her hands unconsciously fingered the ring on her necklace.

Immediately, I knew Adrianna was like me. We were both hurt and damaged due to love. We were like kindred spirits. Hell, I knew I shouldn't have spent too much time listening to Olivia read bedtime stories to her nephew and niece.

"I was five when it started."

Adrianna's eyes flew to mine, but she remained silent.

"My dad started drinking and smoking. I knew my parents loved each other very much. Suddenly, one night, he had hit my mother because of some petty issue.

"Sure, he apologized, but a month later, he hit her again. It continued for years, and I couldn't understand how my father claimed that he loved my mother, but he could hurt her both physically and emotionally. I just couldn't understand it."

"When I was almost fourteen, my father went too far and picked up a knife. He had slashed my mother on her cheek and beat her black and blue until she was hospitalized for six months. Of course, he went to jail. I had to make ends meet and had to do some illegal things to support my mom.

"Scott helped, but it was tough for him, considering he was studying to be a lawyer. Eventually, I learned about illegal cage fighting, and I joined. You could say I joined the wrong crowd. But it was from there I had discovered my love for racing. There were several illegal races in Chicago back then.

"I managed to start anew and did racing as a profession. There you have it, my fucked up childhood."

I didn't know why I just told Adrianna my whole life story. When I was younger, my mother had sent me to a psychologist to help me deal with my childhood. Of course, I didn't say a single word except for a few 'fuck you's' here and there.

With Adrianna, somehow, I could share everything with her. It was most probably that she went through something that hurt her so much. We were like kindred spirits. *Jesus, I sounded like a fool.*

"I can now see why you have some reservations about love. Have you told Olivia about it?" Adrianna said quietly.

I snorted. "Of course not, and I don't intend to."

"Why not?"

I clenched my jaw. "Olivia doesn't need to hear what I've been through and what horrible things I have done. She's raised in a household where things like this don't exist. I don't want her to be aware of it. Mostly, I don't want her pity."

Adrianna shook her head and sighed. "You ought to tell her. Olivia is not naïve. I'm sure she does know about things like what you have been through. Lastly, she would not pity you, in fact, she'll be proud of you. You managed to turn over a new leaf and be who you are today."

I remained silent, not wanting to continue the conversation any longer.

Adrianna sighed and stood up before giving me a small smile. "Think about it. She might surprise you."

Once she left, I shifted my jaw, could I really tell Olivia everything about my horrid past?

I had no fucking clue.

"Hey, you, what's got you so strung up?" Olivia asked as her hands wound themselves around my neck. Her green eyes gazed into mine as she beamed happily at me.

I was momentarily lost for words, and eventually, I shrugged. "Nothing. I was just thinking about some things. Nothing important." I gave a small smile, and she smiled back.

"Okay, wanna head to your place or stay at mine? Just a warning, all of my brothers and my dad will be home today."

I smirked. "Let's go to mine. I'll send you back here tomorrow after breakfast?"

Olivia nodded and grinned. As I followed her out, the question still burned in my mind.

Could I really believe what Adrianna said and tell Olivia what I've been through?

CHAPTER 19-THE GODMOTHER

Olivia

I bit my lower lip.

Ever since Wednesday, Drake had been acting a little distant. Today was Friday, and we had originally planned to go for a date. I bit my lip anxiously. I knew Drake wasn't the marrying sort. And I sincerely hoped that he wasn't acting distant because he wanted to break up with me. My heart ached at that thought, and my stomach felt like it was being twisted from the inside.

"Hey, are you okay? You have been biting your lip and being all… fidgety. I know you well enough that you are scared about something."

I glanced up and gave Adri a distracted smile. "No, I'm just preparing for a date with Drake." With Adri's pointed stare, I spilled, "Okay, I'm just scared that Drake will break up with me. He's been acting really distant since Wednesday. And I know he's not one for a long-term commitment."

Adrianna sighed and shrugged. "He would not break up with you. Trust me. He is most probably having other things on his mind. And he would not break up with you because I threatened him."

I cracked a smile at the end, and she laughed.

"I am serious. I did threaten him. Just enjoy your date. He told me he cares a lot for you though if that makes you feel better."

A small smile graced my lips. "He told you that?" My heart felt like it was going to burst and I couldn't stop the giddy smile on my face.

Adrianna nodded her head and smiled. "Yes, on Wednesday."

"Thank you, Adri." I pulled her into a hug, and she smiled at me. "I don't know what to wear." I shot her a panicked glance when I saw how much time I had left before Drake picked me up.

Adrianna smiled at me before going into my wardrobe. She pulled out a pair of black jeans, a red silk top, a denim jacket, and a pair of flat leather boots.

"Here."

"Thanks." I grabbed the clothes and changed. I bit my lip. "Do I look okay?"

Adrianna nodded and smiled. "You look really good. And I am sure Drake is here already."

I gave her a hug and went down to the driveway where Drake was waiting. The minute Drake saw me, a weird expression crossed his face before he muttered, "You look really… good." His eyes still stuck on my face.

I bit my lip and said awkwardly, "You look good, too."

Immediately, the strange expression was gone, and he smirked. "Let's go." He held me by the waist and led me to his car.

As he helped me get into the passenger seat, I noticed that he was shifting his jaw pretty often. That was one of Drake's signs that he was nervous or anxious. Drake never said it outright, but I caught on pretty quick. Immediately, the worries about Drake wanting to break up with me came back in full force.

"Okay. I guess I've been pretty distant for a while. It's because I've been debating if I should let you meet *her*." Drake admitted after we drove in silence for a while.

At first, I was glad that Drake was not going to break up with me until the word 'her' popped up. I narrowed my eyes. "*Her?*" I swear to God, if Drake was bringing me to meet one of his toys, I was going to raise hell.

"Yeah. Her. My godmother." Immediately, my annoyance faded, and I drowned in confusion.

"Godmother?"

Drake shrugged. "Yeah."

"Oh."

"Just so you know, I don't really want you to meet her because she seems to be on crack twenty-four-seven. And she might scare you away from me."

I laughed. "She can't be that bad." Instantly, I seemed to like this other mother figure in Drake's life.

Drake shot me a flat look. "She's been badgering to meet you. She has not left me alone ever since my mom told her about you."

I grinned. "She sounds really great. What's her name?"

Drake glanced at me before he looked back at the road. "Laura Doukas."

I frowned. "Doukas? That doesn't sound American."

"Yeah, she married a Greek businessman, and they have three children: my best friend, Damien, and his two younger twin sisters, Leila and Sofia."

"Wow, where are we meeting her?"

"A restaurant not far from here," Drake said before giving me a sexy smirk. I smiled, and his right hand grabbed mine before intertwining them.

I held back a cheesy grin at the gesture, and soon we were in front of a classy, sophisticated restaurant.

"Just a warning, if you ever feel uncomfortable, tell me, and we can leave," Drake said as he led me into the restaurant.

I gave him a skeptical look. "There is no way she can be that bad."

"Drake!"

I turned my head to a well-dressed lady in her late forties who threw her arms around Drake and hugged him tightly.

Drake grimaced as he hugged her back gingerly and patted her back awkwardly. "Ugh."

I stifled a laugh, and the lady released Drake before turning to me.

"Oh, you are real!" She gushed before pulling me into a tight, suffocating hug. I let out a squeak, and she released me before beaming.

"Kaitlyn told me about you, and I thought she was playing a prank because I thought, Drake would never get a girlfriend! Believe me, he is such a grouch about it."

"I'm right here," Drake said flatly before sighing deeply. "Olivia, this is Laura Doukas née Hamilton, my godmother. Laura, this is Olivia Ford, my girlfriend."

"Hi, it's really nice to meet you," I greeted, and Laura almost teared up as a beautiful smile spread across her features.

"Oh, she has manners, and she's so beautiful! I'm so proud of you, Drake. She's perfect!"

I blushed at her words, and Drake groaned before gazing up at the ceiling.

"Laura! Knock it off before you scare her away!" Drake grumbled, and Laura rolled her eyes.

"Shut up. You never had a girlfriend before, and I don't think my other son will get one before I'm dead."

Drake muttered curse words under his breath as Laura happily led me to a table with a man sitting there, sipping from a glass.

"Hello, you ass," the man greeted Drake while Drake gave him the middle finger in response. I rolled my eyes and smiled awkwardly at the man.

"Olivia, this is my son, Damien. My husband, Alexander, could not make it. He has some business meeting. My two daughters are off in Paris for some event. All of them sincerely apologize for not being here."

I nodded my head and smiled. "It's okay. Tell them I would like to meet them one day."

Damien smirked at me. I watched him stand up, and he made his way over to me. He kissed my hand and grinned at me charmingly. "Hello, my love."

"Hello. I'm Olivia," I greeted.

Damien was very good looking. However, I found Drake better looking than Damien, probably due to Drake's tattoo.

"Fuck off and stop flirting with my girlfriend," Drake said as he sat across Damien. Damien smirked at him before giving me a wink.

"You—" Drake started.

"Enough, both of you," Laura interjected, and she gave me a wide grin.

Laura fired off questions. "So Olivia, how long have you and Drake been dating? When did you meet? Are you engaged? How many kids do you plan on having? Have you moved in together? And-"

My eyes widened, and Drake interrupted her. "Laura, would you slow down?"

Damien snorted and shook his head. "Mother, let Olivia digest and answer each question before giving her another."

Laura laughed. "Alright. Fine. So?"

"I guess I could say we have been dating for two months," I said as Drake rolled his eyes.

"Three," he corrected, and I frowned.

"Really?"

"Yes," Drake answered shortly.

"Oh. Three it is then."

Laura watched us amused.

I blushed and continued, "No, we are not engaged, and we have not really discussed marriage or kids. No, we did not move in together," I said awkwardly.

Laura grinned wickedly. "Have you had sex?"

My eyes widened, Drake laughed, and Damien groaned.

"Mother."

"Um." That was all I could say before my face flamed. What else could I say?

"Yes. Multiple times. In fact, more than once almost every day," Drake answered with a smirk as he wiggled his eyebrows at me.

Laura laughed and beamed at us. "Does that mean I'll have grandchildren?"

Instantly, I blushed hard, and Drake smirked. "We'll see, but maybe four." My head snapped towards Drake, and I gaped at him. He simply smirked at me.

Laura beamed at us and cooed, "Oh, they're so perfect for each other. Damien! Why can't you find a nice girl like her?"

Damien rolled his eyes and smirked as he winked at me. "Only if Olivia is single, or she has a twin sister." I laughed, and Drake scoffed.

"I am just kidding around. I want to remain single for the rest of my life."

Laura gasped as she leaned against the chairs horrified. "Do you see what I mean? He doesn't even want a girlfriend! Do you think he's gay?"

I choked, and Drake exploded into laughter.

Damien shot Laura a glare. "Mother!"

Laura glared back at him. "You know I'm getting older as each day passes! So get a girlfriend, if not, I tell everyone that!"

Drake continued laughing while I stifled a laugh. Damien muttered some curses under his breath and Laura gave him a triumphant smirk.

"Drake, my darling, you must be very lucky to have Olivia, don't you?" Laura asked, beaming.

Drake looked down at me, and the strange expression crossed his face again. "Yeah, I am," he said with a soft smile on his face.

I smiled back at him, but I couldn't help thinking that *I* was the lucky one to have Drake in my life.

CHAPTER 20-THE

UPCOMING THREATS

Olivia

"Are you serious?"

Lily nodded and grinned slyly. "Yes. Please. I need some alone time with Parker."

I scrunched up my nose. "Gross, I don't want to know what both of you are going to do."

Lily smirked. "So? Just for the afternoon. You can bring them to the mall or something. Just ask Adrianna or Drake to go with you."

I chewed on my lip. "But, I don't know how to handle kids... especially yours."

Lily raised her eyebrows. "Yes, but they're your niece and nephew. I haven't had a good day out with Parker ever since Phillip was born. Sure, we had sex, but those were counted as quickies."

I grimaced. I was quite close to Parker, her husband, and Lily giving me those images of her and her husband getting it on made me nauseous.

"You're just adding those extra details so that I would quickly agree, aren't you?"

Lily shrugged casually. "Maybe."

I sighed. "Fine, fine. I'll bring them to the mall with Adrianna. Drake has some meeting with his manager."

"Great!" Lily beamed and headed to her dresser in her bedroom. "Which is better?"

She held up two pieces of lingerie, and I gagged.

"Bye!" I yelled out loud as I left her bedroom. All I heard was Lily's resounding laughter.

"He is so precious," Adrianna cooed at Phillip in her arms as I held Penny's hand.

I gave her a smile in response before giving my attention to Penny, who was starting to fuss.

"But Aunt Livvy! Mommy always lets me eat ice cream for lunch."

I raised an eyebrow. "Penny, that is not true, and you know that. Besides, we could eat at McDonald's?"

"Okay, fine." Penny pouted before thinking about it for a bit and nodded her head grudgingly. "Aunt Livvy, are you going to have a baby?"

I choked on my coffee, and Adrianna grinned. "What? Penny, why would you say that?"

Penny grinned toothily and stuffed a nugget in her mouth. "Because Mommy said that when people kiss, a baby is formed!"

Adrianna started laughing, and I blinked before I started blushing hard. "No, uh, it's a different kind of kiss."

"Oh, what kind?" Penny asked innocently as she chewed on a fry.

My eyes widened. No way was I going to explain anything about *it* to her. I was going to leave that to Lily. Plus, she was way too young to know anything about that.

I glanced at Adrianna for help, but as the best friend she was, she was ignoring me and feeding Phillip his bottle.

I gave Penny a weak smile before answering, "It means that you have to ask your mom about that because I don't really know the right answer, but your mom does," I said brightly before Penny lost her interest in the subject.

"Why do we have to go to school? School is boring," Penny whined, and I laughed. At this moment, Phillip started fussing.

Adrianna carried him and soothed him before he started wailing. Soon, I watched in awe as he fell asleep with his thumb in his mouth. When Phillip started crying, there was no way you could stop him unless you were Lily or Parker.

"Wow. He's asleep. How did you do that? No one could calm him down unless you're his parents."

Adrianna had a small smile on her face as she gazed down at the sleeping boy. "I do not really know," she said softly as she caressed his cheek.

I gave her a smile. "You'll make a wonderful mom in the future."

Adrianna gave me a tiny smile in return, but her eyes were sad. My heart went out to her, and I felt bad for making her uncomfortable.

"I'm sorry for saying—"

"No. It is okay," Adrianna interjected before giving me a smile. "So how was your date with Drake?"

I sighed dreamily. "It was pretty fun. He brought me to meet his other mother and his best friend."

Adrianna frowned a little before asking, "Wow, that sounds great. Although, I thought he was going to bring you for a picnic."

I raised my eyebrows. "How do you know that?"

Adrianna gave me a smile. "He asked me for advice on how to date you. I guess he must have changed his mind."

"Oh, I see. What did you tell him?" I asked curiously. I hoped she didn't say anything embarrassing about my high school life.

Adrianna opened her mouth to respond before her eyes widened at Penny. Curious, I turned to my left in horror to see that she was using a crayon to draw on the table.

"No, no, Penny! Don't!" I panicked as I pulled her onto my lap. "You can't draw on the tables here, sweetie."

Penny frowned and pouted, her lips pursed. She was about to give me a response when a familiar cold voice spoke up.

"Olivia, I didn't know you'll be here."

I turned around, and the chills went all over my body before I gave him a tight smile. "Hey, um, I had to babysit my niece and nephew."

He glanced at Adrianna before looking down at Phillip and Penny with distaste in his eyes.

Immediately, I wanted to block his view of Penny and Phillip.

"How nice of you," he said coldly, and goosebumps appeared on my skin.

It was so clear that Drew hated children. I gave a weak smile in return, and to my horror, Penny asked loudly, "Aunt Livvy, why does the man have funny hair?"

Drew's face grew even colder, if that was possible.

"Um, Penny, that's not something nice to say. Remember, if you have nothing nice to say, don't say it at all," I said quickly. "So, um Drew, is there something you need?" I asked, hoping that Drew would quickly leave.

"Yes. I would like to speak to you in private," He said, his eyes narrowing in Adrianna's direction. Adrianna gave him a haughty glare before standing up with Phillip and taking Penny's hand in hers and led them away.

"So…" I said awkwardly before trailing off.

Drew sat down before taking my hand. "I would like to invite you out for dinner tomorrow at seven in the evening."

I frowned. Was this guy serious? I am already taken by Drake. "Drew, look, I'm already with Drake. He's my boyfriend. I can't go out with you."

Not that I even want to, I added silently.

Drew's eyes turned cold before he stood up. "You might want to rethink your answer, if not, someone like, let's say, Drake or your family could get hurt."

With that, he left.

I bit my lip. I wasn't stupid. Who was Drew kidding? I was the daughter of the richest man in the world. I had bodyguards at my disposal. Currently, Dan was watching over me, and there was another one watching Adrianna and the children.

There was no way Drew could hurt anyone, not even Drake, considering Drake was stronger than him and tougher as well. I was not going to be like those stupid heroines in books or movies who just blindly follow their blackmailer's orders and somehow, ruins their relationships with those they love. However, I couldn't ignore the threat from Drew. I would have to dispatch some bodyguards for Drake, just to be safe.

I frowned thoughtfully. Drake wouldn't like it, but maybe the bodyguards could watch over him from afar. And if Drew's threat came to pass, they would be there for him.

CHAPTER 21-THE DINNER

Olivia

Mom smiled at me as she sipped from her cup of tea elegantly while my dad shifted his jaw numerous times with a scowl on his face.

"So, how's the weather?" I asked while my mother stifled a laugh and covered her mouth with her hand. Dad opened his mouth to speak, but thankfully, my mother beat him to it.

"Honey, it came to our attention that you and Drake are getting serious—"

"A little *too* serious. Ow!" My dad had interjected before my mother pinched his arm hard.

"And that, we should have *the* family dinner with Drake," my mom continued as if my dad had never interrupted her.

I knew this was coming. I quickly opened my mouth to argue, but my mother narrowed her eyes at me. "No refusals. I expect to see you here tonight at six. The entire family will be there."

I slumped my shoulders, and my dad nodded approvingly.

"Everyone will be here especially your four brothers," he said, very pleased.

Mom rolled her eyes at him. "What am I going to do with you?"

Dad smirked at her before whispering something in her ear that made her blush, and I gagged. My mom was fifty-one, and my dad was fifty-four, but both of them acted like they were still in high school.

My mom glared at my dad, and I shook my head.

"I'm out of here. Fine, I'll see everyone for dinner tonight with Drake," I said reluctantly, much to my parents' approval.

"So, your grandparents will be there, your dad, and your three brothers, and two of them hate me, your inquisitive mother, your matchmaking sisters, your niece and nephew, and my brother. What's there to worry about?" Drake asked casually as he strolled into my home.

I grumbled under my breath. "They're going to ask serious questions about us!"

"So?" Drake replied nonchalantly, and I groaned silently in frustration.

I was worried. *What if my family members asked about marriage and family stuff? Drake and I had not even discussed anything about that kind of commitment. And, what if all those questions made him realize he didn't want commitment at all and decided to break up with me?* I chewed on my lip anxiously.

As we entered the dining room, all eyes swung towards us, some were glares, and others were sly smiles. I gulped nervously.

"Hello, honey. You and Drake can sit here." Mom gestured to two seats in front of her and dad with the rest of my brothers beside him. So technically, Drake and I would be sitting opposite of my dad and brothers.

Oh, the joy.

Drake pulled my chair out for me, and I sat down gracefully, clutching my skirt tightly. Once I was seated, Drake sat down to my left and faced my dad and brothers head on.

And the meal began.

"Drake, technically, how long have you been dating Olivia?" my mom asked as she gave us a bright smile.

"Three months," he answered.

My dad narrowed his eyes. "So, how did you and Olivia meet?"

"She was the stewardess for my cabin in the plane."

"Oh? Before meeting Olivia, how long were you single?" Nathaniel asked as he eyed Drake warily.

"I was single all my life. I never had a girlfriend. I just played around with women, but with Olivia, it's different. I don't mind that she's my girlfriend," Drake answered truthfully, and Ellie and Lily gave him knowing glances and shot me winks.

I turned to my mother to see that she was smiling proudly. That probably meant that she approved of Drake. It was good, but the hard part was my dad and my brothers, excluding Tristan.

"Hmph," my dad mumbled under his breath, and I gave him a kick under the table. He grimaced in pain before giving me a stern look.

Nathaniel raised his eyebrows disbelievingly. "Have you used any of Olivia's money?"

"Shut the hell up, Nate!" I groaned.

Drake shrugged. "No. In fact, I don't need Olivia's money. I have mine. I earn quite a lot from being a professional racer."

"Did you go to college?" Tristan asked curiously.

I shot a glare towards him. "I thought you're not getting involved?"

Tristan frowned. "I'm not. I'm just curious and making small talk."

"No. I did not. At that time, my mother could not afford college for me because my brother just recently graduated. He just started a job. Our family income wasn't enough back then."

I didn't know that. My left hand slipped into Drake's right hand, and I interlaced our fingers together. Drake tensed for a while before he relaxed and held onto mine tightly.

An awkward silence ensued, and my mom asked brightly, "So how do you all find the steak?"

I resisted the urge to drop my head into the plate containing my dinner.

"So, what is your opinion on gender discrimination?"

I rolled my eyes. Three hours have passed, and dinner was over. Still, my dad and brothers had not run out of things to ask Drake.

And the best part? At least half of the questions were irrelevant to Drake and me.

"Gabriel! Stop wasting time on questions that don't concern Drake and Olivia's relationship." My mom chastised, and my dad sulked.

"It is important! What if he treats her badly because she's a girl?"

"Gabriel Xavier Ford!"

"Fine. So, are you and Olivia planning to get married?"

Drake replied casually, "Maybe, but we've only been dating for three months. It's a little too soon to tell."

I gaped at him. I didn't really think he could handle these sorts of questions that involved commitment.

"Humph," my dad muttered disbelievingly.

"So, do you have any kids of your own?"

"Jake!" I snapped, and Drake snorted.

"Of course not. I've never gotten married or had a girlfriend. And I'm always safe, so I don't have any."

Mom gave Jake a glare and smiled at us. "Would you like to have kids one day then, Drake?"

"Ariana! That's my baby girl!"

"Mom! That's our baby sister!"

My father and my brothers yelled, and I could feel myself flush. I groaned inwardly from embarrassment.

This was getting awkward. *Having kids with Drake?* The idea wasn't seem too bad. A little boy with Drake's hair and eyes and his smirk filled me with longing, and I hurriedly pushed that thought away. I couldn't let my thoughts go *that* far.

"Yeah, of course. The idea of having children once made me want to turn around and flee, but with Olivia, the idea doesn't seem so bad," Drake said truthfully, and I melted on where I was seated.

My mom began to beam brightly, and that was the sign she approved of Drake.

"Okay! One last question! It's late." I interjected before my dad continued his interrogation.

My dad frowned and opened his mouth to argue, but my mom nudged him, and he sighed. "Fine. What are your intentions with my daughter?"

"I just want to be with her as long as I can and make her happy."

I turned to Drake. He gave me a heart-warming smile, and I smiled back. I didn't know Drake could be so romantic with his words. Honestly, I never really heard Drake talking about his feelings for me.

My dad looked slightly pleased with Drake's answer, and he nodded his head. My mom stood up and hugged him tightly. "Welcome to the family, Drake," she said in his ear.

Drake seemed surprised by my mom's hug, and he hugged her back. "Thanks."

My mom's actions spurred the rest of my family members to do the same. Tristan went towards Drake and gave him a tap on the back. Lily and Parker were next, followed by Ellie, and then my grandmothers. Jake and Nate followed by giving him another pat on the back.

I let out a relieved breath. I didn't expect this to go so well. Drake seemed overwhelmed too as I guess he didn't expect to be accepted into the family so soon.

"Gabriel?" My mom prompted. My dad sighed heavily and closed his eyes.

"Welcome to the family, Drake." He gave us a short nod before walking out of the room.

My mom beamed at us, and I shot a worried gaze at the direction where my dad had gone.

"Liv, dear, don't worry about your dad. He just needs time to accept that all his princesses have left his castle."

I nodded, and Drake gave me a smirk. He wrapped an arm around my waist and pressed a kiss against my temple.

"Good night, both of you." My mom kissed my cheek before leaving.

I sunk back on the sofa, stunned that everything had turned out amazingly well.

"You okay?"

I smiled up at him. "Yeah, I'm just really surprised that everything went so well, knowing my family."

Drake smirked at me. "Oh, so I did well?"

I stood up and wrapped my arms loosely around his neck, enjoying the feel of the silky soft hair on his nape. I pressed my lips against his own, and he kissed me back hungrily.

I gasped when he bit my lower lip and Drake took the opportunity to slip his tongue into my mouth. He explored every crevice. His hands caressed my curves and roamed all over my body.

When I finally pulled away for air, I told him, "You did everything perfectly." I smiled up at him proudly.

Drake smirked and raised an eyebrow. "Does that mean I get a reward?"

Oh, I know what he meant by reward, and I didn't mind giving it to him. Most probably, I'll be the one being rewarded.

"Maybe. It just depends on how long it takes for you to bring me up to my room," I said teasingly, but Drake took it as a challenge as he tossed me over his shoulder and hurriedly made his way to my room.

I couldn't believe how everything seemed to be falling in place.

And I was right, in the end, I was the one feeling rewarded.

CHAPTER 22-THE

REALISATION

Olivia

"But why did the princess and the prince get to live happily ever after?" Penny asked, frowning as she scrunched up her nose.

"Because he fought the dragon for her," I answered patiently.

"So? What if she doesn't love him?"

I gaped at Penny's logic, which seemed pretty darn reasonable for a five-year-old. It was an extremely shocking and terrifying moment. *What kind of five-year-old doesn't believe in happily ever after?*

Drake sighed. "Well, too bad for her. She has to suck it up and be with him."

I shot a horrified gaze to Drake, who seemed pretty satisfied with the answer he came up with, the smug smirk on his face giving his expression away.

Penny pursed her lips, crossed her arms, and gave in. "Fine. Can we read another one?"

I shrugged and nodded. "Okay, which story do you want?"

Right now, Drake and I are babysitting Penny and Phillip as Lily and Parker wanted another 'alone time' for themselves. So, Penny decided she wanted to read stories, and Phillip decided he wanted to pass out in Drake's arms. I thought it was pretty easy until Penny started asking her questions.

"I want *Snow White and the Seven Dwarfs*," Penny demanded, and I took the book out of the bookshelf.

"Okay, quickly read it. I still have to cook your meals because your Aunt Livvy can't cook to save herself."

"Okay." Penny agreed, and I read the story quietly.

Drake began rocking Phillip to sleep when he almost woke up, and my heart melted. Seeing Drake with a child filled me with longing.

If Drake kept this up, I could fall for him easily.

"So, what are we doing up here?" I laughed as Drake pulled me onto his apartment's rooftop.

Drake gave me a small smirk. "I'm going to tell you something."

"About what?"

"My past. It's...something I haven't told anyone except Adrianna," Drake admitted, and I frowned.

"Adrianna?" I echoed, feeling a bit hurt and confused. *Why did Drake confide in her first?*

"I told her because she could tell that something had happened to me, and she encouraged me to share it with you. The thing is, I had little to no intention to tell you anything about it because I don't want you to pity me, and I hope your views on me won't change."

"Okay. Let's hear it," I said, watching Drake's expression. His body was rigid with tension, and his face was solemn and serious. It was the first I've seen him this serious.

"Before I was five, many people called our family the perfect American family: two kids and loving parents. But when I was five, my father started drinking heavily and doing drugs. He hit my mother because of any petty issues that were there. Of course, after that, he apologized profusely, but after a month later, it started again and soon, it became a regular occurrence."

My eyes widened in shock. I suspected something like that along the lines, but I didn't expect it to happen to Drake at such a young age. I gently reached for Drake's hand and intertwined our fingers. In response, he held mine tightly.

"He would slap or kick her around, and I didn't understand it because, before that, he loved my mother.

How could he abuse her when he loved her? I guess that's why now I don't believe in love at all," he said.

My thumb began stroking his hand comfortingly, and Drake continued with a hard tone, "This went on for years. Occasionally, my father would hit Scott or me, but not to the extreme where he abused my mother. When I was reaching fourteen, my father went too far and slashed my mother with a knife."

I inhaled sharply, horrified. That explained a lot about the scar on Kaitlyn's cheek.

"The police came just in time, and my father went to prison. My mom was sent to the hospital to recover for six months. Because my father was the sole breadwinner of the family and there was no one paying the bills, Scott and I had to find jobs to pay off all the bills, including my mother's hospital fees.

"It wasn't easy, but we did it. After the six months, my mother was released, and things got a little easier until Scott had to go to college. His tuition fees were expensive, and we struggled. I'm not proud to say that I had done a lot of illegal things to get the money we needed.

"When I was fourteen, I joined a gang. I was the errand boy, so to speak. I earned enough to help all of us cover our expenses. I helped deal drugs, fight with others, and robbed, and other illegal stuff. But I never killed anyone." Drake paused, as if afraid he'd scared me.

"Continue," I urged softly, and Drake sighed.

"When I was eighteen, I discovered illegal racing, and I excelled at it. At twenty-two, a scouting agent was there and recruited me. After that, I left the gang and became a professional racer. Since then, I've been able to support my mother, and Scott is a lawyer, so we get by pretty well now," Drake finished. He became silent and shut his eyes. "Let me hear it."

I frowned, confused. "Hear what?"

"That you're going to break up with me."

"What? Why would you think that?" I said, a little confused and hurt.

Drake glared at me. "Because you wouldn't want to be with someone as damaged as me. If you did, you'd be with me because you pity me, and I don't want that."

I shook my head and tugged him nearer to me. "Hey, no, don't think that. I want to be with you because I like you, and I care for you. You think you're damaged? I think you're brave and strong. You survived living with your father for so long. You think I pity you? I'm proud of you. You turned over a new leaf and became who you are today. And I admire you so much, you've made it through hell, and you're still standing proud and tall today. I think you're the strongest and bravest person I know," I said gently.

Drake gazed at me, his blue eyes becoming glassy and he pulled me to him and hugged me tightly. I hugged him back, enjoying his scent on his shirt and the way his muscular arms were wrapped around me tightly.

I pulled away and kissed him on his lips gently. His lips caressed mine softly, and his tongue swept across my lower lip. My hands slid up his shirt and clutched his shoulders tightly.

This kiss was different compared to the others we usually shared. It was filled with comfort, and it was to be savored, not like the passion fueled that lead to us in bed.

Slowly, he pulled away, and he gave me a heart-melting grin. He lay down on the ground and rested his head on my lap, and I ran my fingers through his hair rhythmically. We watched the starry sky together.

And then I realized I wasn't falling in love with Drake, but I was already in love with him.

CHAPTER 23-THE CAR WRECK

Olivia

> *I am in love with Drake Henderson.*
>
> *I am in love with Drake Henderson!*
>
> *Oh god, I am in love with Drake Henderson. Should I tell him? But what if he doesn't feel the same way as I do?* I chewed on my lip and met Adri's pointed stare. We were having a long catch-up session in my room where I must have drifted off in my thoughts.

"Come on, Olivia, I know you are not telling me something during the date between you and Drake."

I looked up at her and shifted nervously. "I-I-I think I'm in love with Drake!" I said quickly.

Adrianna gasped and beamed brightly while her fingers unconsciously played with the necklace containing the ring. "That is good, what did he say?"

I hit the bed with a loud thump and moaned in my pillow. "I didn't say anything to him. He said he doesn't believe in love! I couldn't just tell him that after he said everything about his past."

Adrianna frowned. "Oh."

"What do I do, Adri? I want to tell him, but I'm afraid he doesn't feel the same way." I sighed, and I slumped my shoulders in defeat.

Adrianna raised her eyebrows and said thoughtfully, "You should tell him. What is it that you Americans always say? Yes, 'Go Big or Go Home.'"

I barked out a laugh, and she gave me a grin before I turned serious again. "Really?"

Adrianna nodded. "Yes. Telling him you love him and him telling you he loves you back will be one of the greatest things you will ever feel. I am very sure he cares deeply for you if he was willing to tell you about his past even though he is afraid that you will leave him."

I blinked and sighed. "Yeah."

"Look, is it not better to love and lost than never love at all?" Adrianna asked quietly.

She was right. Adrianna was right. I couldn't imagine life without Drake these past few months. He had made such a big difference in my life. I would never take it back. He made me believe that love was possible... especially for me!

"You're right! I have to tell him!" I burst out to Adrianna, who grinned at me in response.

"Tell who what?" Drake asked curiously as he entered my bedroom.

My eyes widened, and I swallowed nervously. Now that Drake was here, I've seemed to lose all the courage I had gathered from Adrianna's pep talk.

Adrianna gave me a wink as she smiled at Drake before leaving. He gave her a nod of acknowledgment and turned back to me.

"I-I, um… Uh." I stammered, and Drake shot me a pointed stare.

"Who's the guy you have to say something to?"

"I— I…"

Drake narrowed his eyes at my hesitation.

Damn it, where had my guts gone?

"Are you seeing someone else behind my back?" he asked stiffly, and he turns away from me. "Of course, you are. You've probably realized you could do so much better after you heard the sob story of my fucked up childhood."

"Of course not!" I snapped at him and glared at him. "I wanted to tell you that I love you!" I shouted.

It was only when I was met with silence and Drake's stunned expression did I realize what I had done or, *well*, said.

"What?"

Well, that was certainly not the response I was expecting.

"I love you, Drake. I'm in love with you." I repeated hesitantly.

Drake simply blinked at me, looking shocked beyond words.

"Drake, say something. Please," I begged.

Drake still had the same stunned expression on his face, and he started shaking his head. "Olivia, I-I-I can't do this."

And with that, he walked out of my room.

My heart seemed to plummet to the bottom of my stomach. The back of my eyes started to burn, and I knew the tears would start flowing any second right now. I couldn't be here. No, I didn't want to be here.

I choked back a sob and stumbled out of the room. It felt as if my world had come crashing down and everything good was gone. Who knew rejection like this hurt so much? Was this how heartbreak felt like?

I knew I wasn't thinking straight, but at that moment, I couldn't care less. In the current state I was in, I knew I should not be driving but I threw all caution to the wind and got into my car before driving like the hounds of hell were after me.

My heart felt like it was going to split into two, and my throat began to burn. The familiar feeling of the stinging in my eyes started, and the hollow ache in my chest didn't help, and I knew I was close to a breakdown. However, before I could do anything, something crashed into my car, and I found myself spinning rapidly before a loud resounding crash sounded.

Glass exploded and shattered all around me, and everything soon turned blurry. I knew I've gotten into a car accident, and I hoped I was going to die and then I would haunt Drake. I looked around on the empty streets and frowned, I realized I was upside down. The car had probably flipped over several times, and I knew I had to have cuts or injuries and that I should be in pain. However, all I felt was numbness. Physically, I certainly didn't feel anything.

It was pathetic, I know, wishing death on myself because of a man. But I'd rather die and feel nothing after than live with this gut-wrenching pain for the rest of my life.

I shut my eyes and opened them one last time as consciousness was threatening to leave me. The last thing I saw was a pair of black leather shoes walking towards me before I blacked out.

CHAPTER 24-THE REGRET

Drake

It has been four days since I told Olivia about my childhood, and I was still surprised that she hadn't left me that day. *Adrianna was right. Olivia did surprise me.*

I was walking towards her bedroom when I heard Olivia exclaim, "You're right! I have to tell him!"

I frowned as I entered. "Tell who what?" I asked curiously.

Adrianna gave Olivia a wink, and she smiled at me before leaving.

"I— I um… Uh." Olivia paled, and she stammered.

I shot her a pointed stare. "Who's the guy you have to say something to?"

"I— I…" she stuttered and looked at me with wide eyes.

I narrowed my eyes. I knew it. It was too good to be true. Olivia wouldn't stay with me. She had probably realized what a fuck-up I was and that she could do so much better. Most probably, she had moved on already and found someone better. At that thought, my fists clenched together, and I cursed whoever the bloody fucker was.

"Are you seeing someone else behind my back?" I asked stiffly, and I turned away from her. "Of course, you are. You've probably realized you could do so much better after you heard my sob story of my fucked up childhood," I muttered bitterly.

A hand reached my shoulder, and she turned me around before snapping at me. "Of course, not!" I faced Olivia's glare head-on as she shouted, "I wanted to tell you that I love you!"

I couldn't believe it. She must have said something else. *Not that! Yeah. I must have heard her wrong. Most probably, she'd said that she loathed me.*

"What?" That was all I could say as I stared at her, stunned.

Olivia looked at me as she clutched her dress. "I love you, Drake. I'm in love with you," she said hesitantly.

I blinked. *She did say it. She loves me.* I stared at her, shocked. I couldn't believe it. What could she see in me that made her love me? I'm sure I wasn't that special. There were probably millions of guys out there in the world who were better than me and deserved Olivia way more than I did.

"Drake, say something. Please." Olivia begged, and I hated the fact that she was begging for an answer that I didn't even know. Olivia shouldn't even be begging for anything in her life. She didn't deserve an asshole like me who made her beg.

I opened my mouth to reply, but nothing came out. My jaw stopped working for a while, and I'm pretty sure I look like a fucking deer caught in the headlights of a speeding car. Could I give her an answer I don't even know?

Without thinking, I started shaking my head as I slowly backed away from her. Olivia's face fell as if she knew what I was going to say. "Olivia, I-I-I can't do this."

I hurriedly turned away and walked out. I needed space and time to think, but all I could see was Olivia's crestfallen face as I left.

I quickly got into my car and drove off. I sped through the almost empty streets of New York. Suddenly, out of the corner of my eye, I caught sight of a signboard.

Immediately, my heart felt like it stopped and I did an illegal U-turn before parking my car at some random spot near the sidewalk and simply stared at the shop.

Tiffany & Co.

Was I doing what I was thinking? Did I love Olivia? But love doesn't exist. Or does it? Olivia's parents were in love with each other, so were Lily and Parker and my brother and Ellie. Was I in love with Olivia?

Maybe, I didn't know. Could I picture spending the rest of my life with her? The answer was yes. I could.

Could I start a family with her? An image of a little girl who was an exact replica of Olivia flashed through my mind, and I yearned for it to be real. Yeah, I could start a family with Olivia. What I told her family was true. I never had considered starting a family with anyone before until I met Olivia.

Would I be able to want anyone else? No, I didn't and couldn't. There was only one Olivia in this world, and no one else could replace her. No one else had her laugh, her blush, her smile, or her way of brightening up a room when she entered. She was my own personal ray of sunshine.

Was Adrianna right? Was I in love with Olivia all along and just didn't know it? Whatever the case, I wanted to be with Olivia for the rest of my life.

I got out of the car and walked into the jewelry shop. Instantly, I caught sight of an engagement ring that was just simply meant for Olivia.

The silver band of the ring was delicate and was lined with diamonds all over it. A bigger diamond sat in the center of the ring with two slightly smaller ones on each side of it. It was perfect for Olivia.

I paid for it, and the ring was wrapped in the signature blue box. I took it and left.

Now that I was sure as hell that I was going to propose, what the fuck was I going to say?

As I entered the Ford's mansion, I noticed that it was eerily quiet until I heard a loud wail echoing in the house and it sent chills down my spine. Entering the lounge,

I was met with the sight of Olivia's parents sitting on a couch with two police officers in front of them.

What caught my attention was that her mother was sobbing while her father was furious.

"What do you mean my daughter is missing?" Gabriel bellowed, and I entered cautiously.

Ariana caught sight of me before she gasped and continued sobbing. "Olivia is missing."

Immediately, my blood froze in my veins, not being able to believe what I was hearing. "What do you mean missing?"

Olivia's father was now arguing loudly with the police officers, but all I could focus on was the way her mother was crushed.

"She was in a serious car accident, but her body is nowhere to be found. The police called and checked, but she wasn't admitted to any hospitals in New York."

"What?" I sputtered, shocked. I grabbed one of the officers by his collar and shook him. "Where the hell is she?"

"I swear, I don't know. When we got there, the car was in a wreck, but her body wasn't there. We checked the traffic cameras, but the accident was out of range of the cameras."

"Fucking find her!" I shouted as I released the policeman roughly.

How the hell was this happening? I ran my hands through my hair. Panic clogged my throat, and it felt as if someone had punched me in the gut, and I snarled angrily.

This was my entire fucking fault. If I hadn't left Olivia alone, she wouldn't be hurt or injured and missing. *Christ, I was a fucking asshole.* I gritted my teeth, and a thought occurred to me. What if Olivia was dead?

My chest exploded into pain, and I gasped. I couldn't think like that. I had to find her! It was my entire fault that things were like this. My right hand sank into my pocket where Olivia's engagement ring was. I clutched it tightly as I took deep breaths to calm my thoughts.

If she ever accepts it and agrees to marry me, I would spend the rest of my life making it up to her and cherishing her as she should be. Suddenly, I remembered Adrianna's questions.

Would you do anything for her if she asked? Yes.

Would you take a bullet for her? Or would you kill for her? Yes, and once I find who took Olivia, I swear on my life, I would kill him even if I have to die to do so as long Olivia would be safe and alive.

If Olivia left you for someone else, would you let her go willingly because that would make her happy? Yes, if it made her happy and even though I will be left with a broken heart for the rest of my life where I will eventually commit suicide.

And I realized I was in love with Olivia, and it was all my fucking fault that she was gone.

CHAPTER 25-THE PROPOSAL

Olivia

I blinked my eyes open and hissed. My head hurt, and the pounding felt like someone was hitting my head with a hammer. Slowly raising my hand to touch my forehead, I winced as a sharp pain tore through my arm. My eyes widened as I could feel a cut on my forehead.

What the heck happened?

I carefully sat up, wincing the entire time as my body was really sore. My arms were littered with bruises and small cuts. Looking around, I didn't notice the room that I was in.

Suddenly, everything came back to me, and the hollow ache in my chest came back. I gasped as I clutched tightly at my chest as if that very action could ease the pain.

Drake had just walked out on me, and I was in a car accident. *Am I dead?*

No, I was still in pain. I don't think when you die, you're still in pain. I winced as I tried to stand up. *Where the hell am I?*

The room had elegant furniture, and I guessed I was in a hotel room. *How did I end up here?*

Suddenly, the door opened, and I shrunk back towards the four-poster bed.

"I'm sorry for the accident, Olivia. That was not my intention. However, you being here is…"

"You were responsible for my accident? Why am I here, Drew?" I frowned.

I watched warily as Drew faced me head on. His face was expressionless as he shrugged. "You took my warning seriously. You increased security for everyone except yourself. Imagine how easy it was to bring you here."

"You mean, kidnapped me," I said flatly.

"If you put it that way, yes, I kidnapped you."

"Why am I here, Drew?" I repeated carefully. My every nerve was poised to react quickly. Right now, I felt like the prey while Drew was the predator.

He narrowed his eyes and observed me. "My family is going bankrupt, and we can never live like commoners. It is up to me to marry into a rich family so we can maintain our lifestyle."

I paled. I know what Drew was implying. "I won't do it," I said, shaking my head profusely as I backed towards the wall. "I won't marry you, Drew. I don't love you."

Drew's eyes turned cold before he took out a sheet of paper and handed it to me. "This is a marriage license that you and I have to sign. I sincerely hope you are not interested in children because I do not want any."

I crumpled the paper before shredding it into pieces. "I am serious, Drew. I will not marry you. I'm in love with Drake, and I won't marry someone I don't love."

"It has been four hours since you were missing, and no one has been looking for you, especially Drake. Do you really think he cares for you?"

Did Drake really care for me? I didn't know. I wished I knew because I wanted to be with him now, away from this situation. I wanted to be in his arms where I would be safe.

"Yes. He'll come for me," I answered bravely, and Drew clenched his jaw, and a muscle under his right eye twitched.

"Don't make this difficult for yourself Olivia." He produced another copy of the marriage license and passed it to me. "Sign it!" He snarled dangerously.

I shook my head. "No!"

My eyes widened when Drew took out a gun. "Sign it, or I will shoot you right here and right now."

"Shoot me then. You can't make me sign that agreement when I'm dead," I said bravely.

Drew's eyes turned dark, and he threw the gun onto the ground. "Fine. You wanted this to be difficult. Even though I don't want children, I didn't say that this marriage of ours is only in name."

My eyes widened at that statement, and before I could react, Drew grabbed my arms and pulled me towards the bed, and I trembled with fear. I knew exactly what Drew meant. His grip on me tightened as he threw me onto the bed. I whimpered in pain as I landed on my bruised limbs.

"Drew, stop! Please!" I begged as he climbed on top me. Tears of fear and frustration ran down my cheeks as I tried to push him off me. Unfortunately, he was too heavy, and he pulled his jacket off before throwing it to the ground.

"This is your fault, Olivia. Things didn't have to be this difficult, but you left me with no choice," Drew said cruelly as he ripped my skirt.

"Please, Drew, I don't want this!" I begged as he placed wet kisses on my neck. His hands began to wander all over my body, and I cringed in disgust. "Please stop!" I cried out loud as his hands roamed towards my inner thighs.

I didn't want to be with Drew this way. The only man I wanted was Drake. I struggled furiously, determined not to give into Drew.

"Stop struggling!" he shouted as he held both my hands with his right hand.

I could feel his swollen member against my thigh, and I shut my eyes. "Drake! Help!" I screamed.

Drew laughed cruelly in my face. "Drake won't come for you, Olivia. No one will."

"Drake, please!" I screamed again as Drew nudged my thighs apart and positioned himself. I gave one last attempt to kick or hit him, and suddenly, the door burst open, and Drew was pulled off me.

"Drake?" I whispered, not believing my eyes. He was standing in front of the bed, looking at me. Relief was clear in his eyes, but soon, murderous rage replaced them.

"Olivia." That was all he had said before I rushed into his arms.

"Drake!" I sobbed as all the emotions I had felt crashed over me.

Drake hugged me tightly as he caressed my back soothingly. "Shhh, don't worry, everything is going to be fine."

Drake's arms around me tightened as Drew stood up. "Get out, Henderson, or I would shoot Olivia."

The gun! I had forgotten about it! I looked up in fear as Drake clenched his jaw before suddenly tackling Drew to the ground. Drew was too surprised by Drake's sudden movement to shoot him.

I watched in frozen horror as Drake landed blow after blow onto Drew until Drew punched him in the gut. That very punch left Drake breathless and Drew got the upper hand.

Drew landed brutal kicks to Drake's torso, and I screamed, "Drew, stop please!" Drake was on the ground groaning in agony, and it tore my heart to see the man I love in pain.

Drew turned to me and picked the gun up with a crazed look in his eyes. "If I can't have you, no one can!" He began to raise the gun towards me, and I froze in fear.

The gun sounded off, and I screamed as Drake suddenly pulled me down with him.

Drew let out a crazed laugh before shooting himself in the head. I shuddered. Looking at Drew's dead body on the ground reminded myself that I was, at least, one second from being dead.

"Drake," I said in relief before I paled in horror.

"Olivia!" He gasped as he clutched his chest in pain. A dark red splotch started to appear on his shirt, and I collapsed to the ground in shock.

Drew had shot Drake.

"Drake? No. Please." I begged as Drake started coughing up blood. I kneeled down beside him and cradled his face. "Drake?"

"Olivia, I love you. I'm sorry for everything." Drake's eyes looked frail.

Tears continued to flow, and I sobbed. "I love you too, Drake. Don't leave me, please. It's not your fault. It's mine." I held his hands, and he tightened them.

"Olivia!" my dad shouted before running towards us. "Oh no," he muttered as he caught sight of Drake and started to dial for the ambulance.

Drake weakly searched for something in his pocket, and when he took it out, I wept even harder. "Olivia, w-would you be my wife?"

"O-of course, yes, as long as you don't leave me," I answered as tears rolled down my cheeks.

Drake raised a shaky hand and wiped my tears away. "Don't cry. I'm alright." He was lying, and we both knew that he was not all right.

He slowly slid the ring onto my finger, and I gave him a watery smile. "It's beautiful, Drake. I love it."

Drake gave a short laugh before choking and coughing up more blood. "I love you, Olivia. At least, the last thing I see will be your face. The face of the first and only woman I love."

My right hand ran through Drake's hair as his head rested on my lap while my left hand cradled his face tenderly and gently. Drake lifted a weak hand and held my right hand tightly.

"Don't say that," I pleaded, and Drake gave me a short smile.

More tears spilled from my eyes and down my cheeks, and I pressed a kiss against Drake's lips. "I love you too, Drake... so much."

Drake smiled at me weakly before he murmured, "I love you, Olivia." After which, his hands went slack, and his eyes closed shut.

CHAPTER 26-THE COMA

Olivia

I clutched Drake's limp hand and rubbed soothing circles on his palm.

"Livvy, dear, you have to eat something," my mom said gently, and I shook my head.

"No. I'm not hungry."

"I don't think Drake would want you to starve—"

"You don't know what he wants, okay?" I said sharply, and my mom sighed.

"Alright." She left the room.

It has been a week since the incident and Drake was admitted to a hospital. However, he was in a coma due to extreme blood loss, and I have not left his side ever since. When Kaitlyn had seen her son lying in the hospital bed motionless, she burst into tears. Surprisingly, Vincent had visited Drake before going back to London three days ago.

I sighed before catching sight of the engagement ring on my finger. If only Drake were awake, we would be celebrating our engagement like any normal couple. The ring on my finger seemed right like it was always meant to be there.

My gaze ran over Drake's face. Most of his bruises were gone, and the bullet hole in his chest was healing nicely. I sighed anxiously. What if Drake was in a coma for the rest of his life? I bit my lip at that thought before straightening my resolve.

No! I couldn't think that way. I must stay positive. I had to. If... I mean, when Drake wakes up, we would get married and have scads of children, okay, maybe three, and we would live happily ever after.

I sighed, biting my lip as tears threatened to fall. I stroked Drake's stubbled jaw. I missed him. I missed Drake. I missed his kisses, his smirk, his dry humor, his smile, his scowl, the way his arms fit perfectly around me. God, I even missed his sexual innuendos! In all, I just missed him. I wanted to tell him I love him and for him to say it in return.

A hollow ache filled my chest. I couldn't lose Drake. I could not. If I did, I wouldn't have any reason to live anymore. My world seemed dark, and I could feel sorrow and grief sinking in. I lay my head on his chest, and I wept for things that could have been.

"Livvy, wake up. The doctor wants to see you in five minutes."

I rubbed my eyes blearily as I sat up straight. "No changes?"

Nate gestured towards Drake's unconscious body. He gave me a sad smile, and I looked away. "None." I fingered the ring, and Nate asked, "So he proposed?"

"I thought everybody knew already," I answered tonelessly, my eyes fixed on my fiancé's body.

Nate sighed before sitting. "They did. They just didn't know when he proposed."

"It was when he was on the ground bleeding from the bullet wound."

Nate looked taken aback by my answer, and he didn't seem to know what to say.

Feeling a little guilty for making him feel uncomfortable, I asked, "How did Drake and dad find me, anyway?"

Nate shot me a guilty look. "I had a tracer on you. I overheard you talking to the guards to increase them for everyone. I was suspicious, but I didn't want to confront you about it, so I placed a tracer on you."

I looked at him emotionlessly before turning my gaze back to Drake. "Oh."

"Liv, Drake wouldn't want you to be in this state. You're barely eating or sleeping."

I glared at him. "I wish everyone would stop telling me what Drake would want for me! You don't know him that well! What makes you so sure that you know what he wants from me?"

Nate sighed. "I may not know him well, but I'm sure he wouldn't want to see you like this."

I opened my mouth to argue, but the door opened, and Drake's doctor came in. "Miss Ford, there are certain things that we have to discuss about your check-up from a few days ago."

I sighed tiredly. "Okay, discuss away."

"Are you sure? What we have to discuss is something that you might want to be in confidential." The doctor shot Nate an uncomfortable glance.

I shook my head. "Just say it."

"The test we took from you shows that you are pregnant, but your weight and your lack of—"

"Wait, what?" I said disbelievingly.

"My sister is pregnant?" Nate looked like he was going to have a heart attack.

"Well, yes, the baby would be about three weeks," the doctor answered.

"A baby?" I gasped and looked down at my flat belly.

"Yes. A baby. Seeing that now you're an expectant mother, you have to put on more weight. Currently, you are now severely underweight. If you continue, you would have a miscarriage."

A miscarriage? No way in hell. I couldn't lose Drake's baby. I could be losing Drake, but I couldn't lose his baby too. "What do I have to do?"

The doctor peered at me before looking back at his clipboard. "Well, you have to eat more regular meals and be well rested. Contain your emotions properly like staying away from stress, and you and the baby will be all right."

"Okay. Thank you," I said, stunned. I had a baby in me. A part of Drake and a part of me is growing inside.

The doctor nodded and left, and Nate bursts out. "He got you pregnant? Both of you have been having se—" He cut himself off and said sheepishly, "I mean, um… wow! Congratulations!" He left hurriedly, leaving me alone with Drake.

I ignored him and caressed my belly with a smile. I am pregnant with Drake's child! My world didn't seem so bleak anymore. I had a reason to live again.

"I'm pregnant, Drake, with your child. Please wake up soon," I said softly and held Drake's hand. I pressed a kiss on his lips, and my stomach rumbled.

"I'll be going down to the cafeteria to grab some food for our child. I'll be back soon." I stroked his cheek and left.

CHAPTER 27-THE REUNION

Drake

I jerked awake. *Fuck, I felt like I was run over by a truck.* I looked around and frowned. *Why the hell was I in a hospital?* My whole body ached and as I slowly sat up and winced. My chest hurt like hell.

I gingerly touched my chest and felt the bullet wound, and everything came back to me.

Shit. Where was Olivia? Was she okay? I had to make sure. I winced as I got out of the hospital bed and pulled off the needles that were embedded in my skin. I leaned against the bed and limped in pain towards the door when the heartbeat machine made a long beep sound as it flatlined.

Immediately, a doctor and a few nurses rushed into the room and breathed out a sigh of relief when they saw me.

"What the fuck are you looking at?" I demanded, annoyed.

"Just making sure you stayed alive, Mr. Henderson. If not, all the Fords would come after our necks." The doctor gestured to himself and the nurses.

I didn't care about them. What I wanted to know was where Olivia is. "Where's Olivia?" I demanded and shrugged away from a nurse who tried to bring me back to the bed.

"Mr. Henderson, please. You shouldn't be moving too much, given your current condition. You need all the rest you can get," the doctor pleaded.

I growled in response. "I'm not doing a damn thing until you tell me where Olivia is!"

The door burst open, and Olivia rushed in, frightened and panicky. "What's happening? A nurse said that the heartbeat machine flatli... Oh, Drake!" She gasped, and her hands covered her mouth, tears fell from her eyes and rolled down her cheeks, and I was pleased to note that they were tears of relief and not sadness.

Immediately, she ran into my arms and sobbed. "Oh, Drake, you're awake! You really are awake!"

Seeing her alive and well in my arms made me let out a sigh of relief. The adrenaline in my body faded, and I would have crumpled to the ground had it not been for Olivia and a nurse tugging me gently to the hospital bed.

"What do you mean awake?" I asked, confused.

Olivia sniffled. "You've been in a coma, Drake... for a week since the incident."

"What?" I said disbelievingly. I had been in a coma?

Olivia nodded and sat in the chair beside the hospital bed. She stroked her fingers against my cheek, and I closed my eyes. God, I missed her. Her touch on my skin felt like heaven to me. No one else could make me feel this way like Olivia did.

I opened my eyes as Olivia continued to caress my hand soothingly as if she was trying to make sure that I was really awake and not a figment of her imagination.

I observed her quietly. Olivia had become skinnier. I frowned. Olivia was slim enough. She didn't need to be any skinnier, and I liked her body just the way it had been before, not skinny like the models I had screwed around with. Olivia's face had become more tired, and she had dark circles under her eyes. She was definitely not getting enough sleep, most probably due to worrying about me.

Guilt pooled in my stomach, and I clenched my jaw. I hated the fact that I was the cause of her current state.

"I'm sorry for interrupting your reunion, Miss Ford, but I have to check up on Mr. Henderson's vitals," the doctor said uncomfortably.

I growled. "Too fucking bad, get the hell out."

"It's okay, Drake." Olivia gave a smile to the doctor and the nurses, and she moved away. "I'll call your mom and your brother. They'll be glad to know that you have awakened."

When the doctor and nurses finished prodding me, they left quickly, and Olivia came back to sit beside me. "I thought you'll never wake up." She breathed out, and I gave her a reassuring smile.

"Don't cry anymore, Olivia. I'm awake. Everything will be fine now."

Her fingers interlaced with mine, and I caught sight of the engagement ring I had given her on her finger. The ring fit perfectly and looked like it should have been there the entire time. Instantly, waves of possessiveness and lust crashed over me.

The ring was like a signboard that showed other men that Olivia was taken. It was like a tag on her finger that screamed at others, 'Property of Drake Mitchell Henderson.'

The ring was simply meant for Olivia. It just described her perfectly well. My thoughts wandered to how it would be like to fu—*No*, make love to Olivia where she would be wearing nothing but that ring on her finger. Instantly, I went hard, and I wanted nothing but to take her right here in this hospital room wearing nothing but the ring.

Suddenly, I grabbed Olivia and kissed her hungrily. Olivia moaned softly, and her fingers threaded through my hair while my hands cradled her face. Her lips pressed against mine gently. *God, I missed this*—kissing Olivia. I slowed the kiss and licked her lips before pulling away.

"I love you, Olivia," I said softly but seriously, and I pushed back a blonde curl that had fallen loose behind her ear.

Olivia beamed brightly, and I swear, the room seemed to brighten when she smiled. God, she was fucking beautiful, and she was mine. I felt like the luckiest bastard in the world.

"I love you too, Drake," she said softly and cradled my cheek.

I growled playfully. "I love hearing you say that. Say it again."

Olivia laughed. "I love you, Drake."

I grinned, satisfied. "I knew you would fall in love with me one day." I teased Olivia, and she rolled her eyes and hit me lightly on the arm.

"Drake!"

"Okay. Okay! I love you too, Olivia."

Olivia smiled and gazed off. "I was so scared, Drake. Scared that you would never wake up because I need you, and so does the... um... uh," She stammered and froze.

I narrowed my eyes. "What or who else needs me?"

Olivia's eyes widened. "Um, our child needs you. I'm pregnant."

Olivia is pregnant with my child? A part of me and a part of her is growing in her. My possessive side surged, and my eyes gazed down at her flat belly.

"Really? How long?" A small smile crept onto my face, and the image of the little girl with blonde hair who was a miniature of Olivia flashed into my mind.

"The doctor said three weeks. Are you happy about this baby?" Olivia asked hesitantly.

I frowned, bewildered. "Why not? It's a part of you and a part of me. How could I not love it?"

Olivia's eyes welled up with tears as she threw her arms around me. "Oh, I'm so glad that you're happy about this. I was worried that you wouldn't want the baby and me."

"I want this baby, and I want you. Heck, Olivia, I love you. I'm in love with you, and this baby is a part of you. Of course, I would love it. I'm just hoping it's a girl," I said seriously.

A smile broke out on Olivia's face, and she rained kisses on my face. "I love you so much, Drake, but I hope it's a boy that looks exactly like you." She beamed, and her face fell slightly.

"Drake, even though my parents accept you, they are extremely old-fashioned. They will disapprove if the baby is born before marriage." She winced and said hesitantly as if she was afraid I'll up and leave her as soon as she said the word 'marriage.'

However, I liked the idea. I liked the idea a lot. The sooner Olivia and I got married, the sooner she will officially be mine. *Mrs. Drake Henderson. God, I liked the sound of that. I liked it a lot.*

"Honestly, marriage with you doesn't seem horrible if it would mean you are officially mine. You're the mother of my child, and besides, if I gave you that ring, it means I wanted to marry you way before I knew about our daughter."

I gave her a suggestive smirk. "And I can't wait for our wedding night. You won't be leaving the room for days."

Olivia blushed and rolled her eyes, but I could see the anticipation in her eyes. "You're unbelievable." She gazed at me tenderly and kissed me softly. Her arms wrapped themselves around my neck loosely, and my fingers were tangled in her loose curls.

She pulled away slowly, and I frowned, not happy with the mere kiss. She said seriously, "Just for the record, it's our son." With that, she continued kissing me, and I laughed.

Everything was right in our world again.

CHAPTER 28-THE CONCLUSION

Olivia

Three months later

I lay lazily in bed, too sated to move from Drake's love-making. The silk sheets under me felt cool to the touch. Drake and I were in Italy for our honeymoon. I had never been to Italy, so Drake has decided we would be going there.

Drake had stayed true to his word, and ever since a week ago, we had not left the hotel room.

"Wow, I knew I was good. I just didn't know I was that good."

I rolled my eyes and sat up slowly and grabbed the blankets to cover my body. "Oh shush, we really should leave the room. It's been a week, and I really want to go sightseeing."

Drake smirked. "I've seen every inch of you naked. Why bother covering yourself up?"

I flushed and shot him a pointed glare. "Drake!"

"Fine. We can head out later to see the streets after we have a shower." He gave in and winked at me.

I narrowed my eyes. "No! We'll shower separately. If not, we'll never be getting out of this room."

Drake sighed, defeated. "Fine. Tell me when you're done." He lay on the bed with a pillow over his face. I scoffed and entered the bathroom.

I was now officially Mrs. Drake Henderson or Mrs. Olivia Ford-Henderson or just Olivia Henderson. Either way, the name change sent shivers down my spine. I loved it.

Being married to Drake hasn't changed anything between us. Now, we just lived together in the same house, and we said 'I love you' to each other. Everything was the same.

As I shampooed my hair, I caught sight of the engagement ring and the simple wedding band on my finger. I couldn't help but smile at the memory that came with it.

One week ago

As my dad walked me down the aisle, I couldn't help but stare at Drake. He looked really handsome in his black tux. His hair was untamed, and he didn't bother styling it. I was okay with that. I liked his hair the way it was. From where I was, I could see my mom and Ellie crying as Scott hugged her. Kaitlyn was there and a proud mother she was as she watched Drake and me.

Ellie and Scott's wedding was much grander and elaborate than Drake and mine. We both wanted a small intimate wedding with not much fuss. I was slightly unhappy about being Ellie's bridesmaid because I had to go for another fitting due to the slight growth of my pregnant belly.

As I walked closer to him, I couldn't help but mentally laugh at his stunned expression as he looked at me. His face was filled with admiration, love, awe, and of course, lust.

My wedding dress was strapless and had a sweetheart neckline that hinted at a bit of cleavage. It was form fitting until my waist where it flared out slightly, leaving me room to walk. Lace and bits of diamonds decorated the dress. I was slightly thankful I was not a little over three months. If not, I had to wear a different wedding dress. I was also wearing white ballet flats. Not that anyone could see, but I didn't want to wear heels as my legs would ache, and I was afraid of tripping. My hair was in a loose chignon at the base of my head and had a diamond headpiece to keep the veil in place.

As I reached the end of the aisle, my dad passed me to Drake and gave him a glare before changing it into a small smile. Drake took my hand gently, and we faced the vicar.

Immediately, the vicar started rambling on, and Drake whispered, "You look so fucking hot. I can't wait till I get to strip you out of that dress and have my way with you."

I shot him a horrified look. "You can't swear in a church, Drake," I whispered back to him, and he smirked charmingly at me.

I couldn't help but smile back at him. Finally, the vicar stopped talking and gestured for the rings. Drake and I decided on a simple silver band. Mine had a single diamond on it while his was plain.

After Drake and I had exchanged rings, the vicar announced, "By the power vested in me, Mr. Drake Hen—"

Before the vicar could even finish his sentence, Drake had already begun kissing me. His hands stayed on my waist, and I cradled his face as we kissed gently.

I pulled away and blushed as we faced the crowd in the church. The wedding was simple but classy—the dream wedding I wanted when I was younger. There weren't many people there seeing that I liked that it would be small and intimate.

Drake's best man was not Damien because he couldn't make it due to some urgent matter in Greece. Instead, his friend from Chicago, Slade Kolosov, stood beside him and took the honor.

I was a little intimidated by him at first. He looked like a gangster. In fact, he was the exact stereotype of a gangster. His entire right arm was covered in tattoos, but he was very good looking. Drake had informed me that Slade was and *is* a gangster. In fact, he was the leader of the Russian mob in Chicago.

I warmed up to him immediately when he started telling me that he had helped Drake when they were in their teens and had a lot of dirt on Drake when they were young.

Slade winked at me, and I laughed. "It's still not too late to annul your marriage. You guys have not consummated it yet. You still can leave this fucker and run away with me."

A smile tugged at my lips, and I snorted. "Run away with you? You run away from commitment."

"If I'm a fucker, you're a fuckhead. Stop flirting with my wife," Drake said with a smirk on his face.

Slade gave us a wounded look. "How nice of you two to abuse my ego?" He gave us a solemn look before shrugging and giving us a smirk. "I'm fine with being called a fuckhead. Olivia, my darling, if you ever miss me or get sick of this asshole, give me a call. I'll be waiting." He winked.

I gasped and hit both of their heads. "Stop swearing in church!"

Both of them shared an amused look before bursting into loud laughter. I shot them a flat look, and Drake immediately stopped.

Slade snorted. "You are so whipped."

Drake glared at him. "For today, yes! If not, I'm not getting laid on my wedding day!"

Slade blinked before exploding into laughter, and Drake soon followed. Both of them were so alike in many ways. I shook my head at that and went to greet the well-wishers.

I smiled at the memory before dressing. I was met with a snoring Drake when I exited the bathroom. I rolled my eyes and grabbed a pillow and whacked him with it.

"Hmm? What? I was having a good dream where you and I are naked and—"

"Drake, shut up!" I hissed as my face flamed. He started laughing. I made a face to him and picked up my purse. "Come on, let's go eat. Trevor and I are hungry."

Drake raised an eyebrow. "Savannah is hungry again?"

"Yes, Trevor is hungry now. You kept me up all night, and we're starving. Trevor wants to eat authentic gelato, a strawberry-flavored gelato," I said, smiling as I caressed my baby bump.

Drake smirked and pulled a shirt on. "I told you, it's going to be a girl—Savannah Henderson. It has a nice ring to it." He rubbed the baby bump over my maternity dress.

I laughed and replied, "Trevor Henderson has a nice ring to it as well."

"Whatever the gender is, let's go get lunch and some gelato for our kid," Drake said as he pressed a kiss on my head and gently tugged me to the streets.

Six months later

"Middle name?"

"Kellan," I replied as Adrianna carried my baby.

"That is a nice name. Trevor Kellan Henderson. He looks exactly like Drake. He has your blonde hair, though," Adrianna said quietly as she smiled down at Trevor in her arms.

I watched adoringly as Trevor yawned before trying to stuff his fist in his mouth. "Will it be okay if I appoint you as Trevor's godmother?"

"Of course, that is a really big honor for you to bestow upon me." Adrianna blinked up at me and a smile crossed her face.

I grinned. "That's great to hear. I heard you're going back to Spain soon," I said sadly.

"Yes, I have to go back to work and other things."

I sighed and gave her a smile. "I'll miss you."

Adrianna gave me a smile before gently passing Trevor to me. "I will miss you, too. I have to go and get some items before I leave tomorrow. I will see you tonight."

She gave me another smile before leaving. I looked down adoringly at Trevor and stroked his cheek. The moment I first saw him, I was in love. My mom says I was lucky for I was only in labor for two hours.

Trevor blinked up at me before giving me a toothless grin. My heart melted, and I cooed at him.

"Honey, I'm home!" Drake called out, and I rolled my eyes and smiled. He walked into the room, looking sexy as ever before a grin tugged onto his lips as he gazed at me holding Trevor.

"I can get used to this sight," he said with a small smile on his face. I grinned back at him and passed Trevor to his waiting arms. My heart melted to see Drake with Trevor. It was strange, but seeing Trevor in Drake's arms was unbelievably sexy.

Drake's biceps flexed as he rocked Trevor to sleep, and I couldn't help but be turned on. Watching both of them made my maternal instincts flutter.

"*Whatcha* thinking about?" Drake asked curiously with a smirk on his face.

"How I finally got my happy ending with you," I said with a tender smile.

"I'm glad my happy ending is with you." Drake's smirk faded and was replaced with a genuine smile.

My heart fluttered, and I couldn't help but kiss him lightly on the lips. "I love you, Drake."

"I love you too, Olivia," Drake said and kissed me again.

And I couldn't help but think that even though Drake was really bad for me with his curse words and whatnot, I couldn't be happier that I got my happily ever after with him.

EPILOGUE

Drake

6 Years Later

There were many times I had wondered why I had to deserve such an amazing wife, kids, and the house with all those stupid shit like white doors or something like that, considering I was no saint. But I guessed I must have done something good in my past life to deserve everything I have now.

"So you really think this is a good birthday present to get for a four-year-old?" Damien asked doubtfully.

I looked at him and shrugged. "What's wrong with it? Olivia said it's fine."

Damien raised his eyebrows and gave me a flat look. "I think she meant a toy pony."

"Why would anyone want a toy when you can get the real one? Right, buddy?" I frowned. I patted the white pony who let out a neigh and stomped her hooves. "See, even Snow White agrees."

Damien rolled his eyes and raised his hands. "Whatever, just load the beast into the truck."

"Drake Henderson! I meant a toy pony! Savannah is too young to ride a horse. What made you think I meant a real horse?"

I glared at Damien, who was sniggering at me. "Savvy wanted one, and she kept looking at me with those eyes of hers."

Olivia groaned and shook her head. "Okay. Just send the horse back before she sees it."

"Mommy!"

I smirked at Olivia who let out a frustrated sigh and picked our daughter up. Savannah Henderson was almost a replica of Olivia except she had my eyes.

"Pony!" Savvy shrieked as she wriggled in Olivia's arms to reach for it.

"Happy birthday, princess. Her name's Snow White."

Olivia handed her to me, and I took her eagerly into my arms. Even though it has been four years since my daughter was born, I still couldn't believe that Olivia and I had created her.

Savannah let out a hand to stroke Snow White's mane. "Thank you, daddy! I love you!" She snuggled into my neck, and I could feel the love I had for her spill out of my heart.

Olivia signaled for a helper to bring the pony to the stable. "Where's Trevor?" Trevor was our five-year-old son who looked like me except for his blond hair which he had inherited from Olivia.

"Oh, he's playing with Dalton."

Dalton was Ellie and Scott's son. With Trevor and Savannah, we have our hands full. Trevor was like a mini tornado, creating trouble everywhere he went. Savannah was no different in following her older brother's footsteps.

Because Trevor was born only six months after Olivia and I got married, Olivia's brothers and dad had put two plus two together. As a result, I had received a lot of crap from Olivia's brothers and dad for not keeping my dick in my pants before Olivia and I were officially married.

"Daddy!" I let out an *oomph* as Trevor tackled me to the ground. Thankfully, Savvy was in my arms, and I had managed to not land on her. Savvy squealed as Trevor sat beside her on my body.

"Kids, get off of your dad," Olivia reprimanded. Even though six years had passed, she was still breathtaking, especially when she was all motherly.

Trevor grumbled under his breath and pouted.

"Trevor, go and check if your grandparents are here." Olivia gestured to the doorway. Trevor frowned and reluctantly went back into the house. "Savvy, go into the house. I need to talk to daddy."

"Okay."

I watched Savannah skip into the house from the ground and smirked at Olivia. "So, what did you want to talk about?"

"What are we going to do about the horse?" Olivia sat down beside me. "Savvy won't be able to ride the horse until she's older."

I lifted my head and shifted and rested my head on her lap. Now, my eyes were looking up her chest. "Mmm. That's nice."

"Drake!" Olivia crossed her arms trying to look serious, but her action only made her breasts look fuller.

I groaned as lust overtook me, and I said huskily, "Kiss now, talk later." I reached out for Olivia and crashed my lips against hers. At first, she resisted but eventually gave into the kiss. I kissed her hungrily, and I could feel Olivia getting into the kiss. Her hands were running through my hair, and she was making little moans as I brushed the sides of her breasts through her skin-tight white dress.

"Hey! No PDA in front of me!"

Olivia broke the kiss and ran her fingers through her hair. For me, I was unbelievably turned on. I shifted my head to see Nate glaring at us. Now that Olivia and I were married, Nate couldn't grill me for trying to get it on with Olivia.

"Momma! They're here!" Trevor hollered as he ran past Nate. Olivia sighed and gave me a longing look before reluctantly standing up and picking Trevor from the ground.

"Drake, come on. Get Savvy ready for dinner, and I'll settle my family."

I cast a longing look at Olivia's figure as she went back into the house. It's been days since I got laid because Olivia was always too stressed up or tired from planning Savannah's party.

"Savvy, come on, let's get you ready for dinner." I picked up a squealing Savannah and went to dress her.

I still couldn't believe that Trevor and Savannah were my kids. I loved Savannah and Trevor the moment I had first laid eyes on them in the delivery room.

I grabbed a hairbrush and looked at Savannah in the mirror, she was kicking her feet in the air excitedly. She gave me a toothy grin, and I promptly began brushing her golden tresses.

"Daddy, does Uncle Nate like you?"

I snorted quietly. "Um, yeah." *What was I supposed to say? Oh, he doesn't because I've been screwing your mom before we got married. Yeah, that'll get me in a load of shit from Olivia.*

"Okay." Savannah started humming the tune of *Twinkle, Twinkle, Little Star*, and I put down the brush.

"Okay pumpkin, let's go say hi to everyone." I picked her up and headed down.

When Olivia and I had gotten married, we had decided we didn't want to stay in the Ford mansion like everyone else. Instead, we got a new house as we wanted our privacy. Well for me, I wanted Nate to stop interrupting my nightly routines with Olivia. There had been many disagreements, but as usual, Ariana had stepped in and told us it was up to Olivia and me if we wanted to move out.

Anyone who protested received a glare from her. So, all in all, I did owe Ariana a lot.

"There's my little sweetie! Happy birthday, sweet pea." Leslie cooed at Savannah and took her out of my arms. I shrugged and walked off to find Tristan and Scott. Out of all four of Olivia's brothers, I found Tristan easier to get along with.

"Hey, where's Savvy?" Olivia came up to me.

"Uh, with Leslie. Want to have a quickie?"

Olivia shot me a flat look and slapped my chest. "Drake, behave yourself. My family is here. We can have more than a quickie later tonight. I promise you."

"You better, I need some attention from my wife."

Olivia rolled her eyes, but I could see anticipation and desire in her eyes. She walked off to attend to a caterer, and I was about to follow her when Trevor pulled on my jeans.

"Daddy, I'm hungry."

I picked him up and placed him on my shoulders. "Okay buddy, let's go outdoors." Trevor giggled as I pretended to drop him from my shoulders.

"Ah! There's my cutest little nephew!" Ellie cried out as she pinched Trevor's cheeks. Trevor scowled, and Ellie chortled. "He even has the same scowl as you!"

I frowned. "I don't scowl."

"You're doing it now." Lily smirked.

I huffed and shrugged. "Well, Olivia seems to like this face a lot."

Gabriel grimaced, and Trevor ran to him and begged to be carried. I knew that Gabriel had a soft spot for Trevor, considering he was his youngest daughter's child.

"Granddad! Carry!" Trevor demanded, and I could see he had the impatient quality that Olivia possessed.

Tristan sidled up to me and passed me a beer.

"Thanks."

I took a long swig, and Tristan asked, "Plans to have any more?"

I coughed and sputtered, "What?"

"Plans for any more kids?"

I shook my head and then shrugged. "I don't know. Maybe in the future. Not now, though. I got my hands full. Both Trevor and Savannah are a handful."

"Savannah is a handful? Are you sure? She's like an angel." Tristan laughed.

At this point, Savannah shrieked loudly, earning the attention of everyone in the house and backyard. "No! I don't wanna! I don't wanna!" A loud crash followed after.

"Okay. She's definitely a handful. Thank God, Isla wanted to wait for a while more to have kids," Tristan mumbled, and I snorted.

"Drake! Here you go with Daddy, and I'll clear your mess." A frazzled-looking Olivia passed a frowning and scowling Savannah to me.

"What happened?"

Olivia let out a puff of breath. "She refused to take her milk and threw the cup on the floor."

"Okay. I'll take care of Savvy while you go clean up."

Olivia smiled at me gratefully and kissed me on the cheek. "Thank you, hon."

I smoothed Savannah's hair and frowned at her. "Savvy, you need to behave. Do you hear me? If not, I could send you to your room right here, right now, and you won't be able to enjoy your party."

Savannah nodded her head and buried her head in the crook of my neck. "I'm sorry."

"It's okay. Go play with Ally." I watched Savannah run to where Penny and Ally were.

"You know, you're good for her," Gabriel commented.

"She's my daughter—"

"I meant Olivia. Before she met you, she would be such a worrier, but now that you two are together, she's happier and has lightened up."

I had no idea what to say to that. It was no secret that Gabriel and I did not have the best relationship. "Well, I love her, and I'm thankful to you for bringing such an amazing person like Olivia to the world." I guess being honest was the key to finally winning him over.

Gabriel had a soft smile on his face as he gazed at Olivia. No words were said, and understanding was reached.

Savannah squealed in delight as she opened yet another expensive gift.

It was way past bedtime for her, but she was way too excited to sleep. Trevor had already gone to bed.

"Okay, pumpkin, time to sleep. You can play with your new toys tomorrow."

I watched from the doorway as Olivia put Savannah to sleep. Olivia bent to kiss her good night, and I could feel my jeans getting really tight as all blood flowed south.

Now that I noticed, Olivia was wearing a skin-tight white dress that was now hugging her bottom snugly. I groaned softly. Now, I was painfully hard because there was no one around to interrupt, and I was finally getting laid.

Olivia got up and walked towards me. "You gonna go to bed now?"

I shot her a smirk. "Yeah, with you."

Before Olivia could react, I carried her to our bedroom and tossed her onto the bed. Olivia laughed, and I climbed on top of her.

I chuckled to myself and pulled her to me. Her head was on my chest, and she snuggled closer to me. "You know, Tristan asked me if we had plans for any more kids."

Olivia shot me a warning look.

I continued, "I told him that maybe in the future, not now. But I think we should have another girl and boy for Savvy and Trevor to play with."

Olivia shook her head. "Haha, no way! I can't take care of four kids. I have no idea how my mom took care of seven kids, but I'm not doing it."

I chuckled and traced patterns on her bare waist. "Okay. We'll see."

Olivia rolled her eyes, but a gentle smile came onto her face. "I love you, Drake. You've given me everything I ever wanted in life."

"No, you've given me a family and future I thought I'll never have. Without you, I think my life would have spiraled out of control," I admitted while pushing back a curl of Olivia's hair behind her ear.

Olivia caressed my cheek softly and kissed me soundly. "I love you, Drake, even with your possessive streak. Never ever doubt that."

"I love you so much, Olivia."

"Daddy!" I heard Trevor yell, and I sighed. Olivia shot me a longing look and grabbed her dressing robe and headed off. I grumbled under my breath and grabbed my boxers and followed Olivia.

I leaned against the doorframe to see Olivia carrying a crying Trevor. "There, there, baby, tell mommy what happened," Olivia cooed.

Trevor shook his head vigorously, tears still streaming down his face. "I want daddy!"

"Hey, kiddo." I took Trevor from Olivia, and he calmed down. "Daddy is here. Want to tell me what happened?" I smoothed down his wild black hair.

"T-the clown came after me."

I exchanged amused glances with Olivia. Somehow, Trevor had been having nightmares of clowns chasing after him with balloons. "Well, the clown can't come here because mommy and daddy can help you chase them away."

Trevor shook his head. "No! I wanna sleep with daddy."

I sighed. *There go my chances of getting laid again.* "Okay, buddy. Let's go."

Olivia led the way while Trevor absentmindedly played with my hair. Olivia slid on a shirt and undies before climbing into the bed. "Come on, buddy. Climb under the covers."

Trevor eagerly slid under the covers and snuggled between both Olivia and me.

"There. Now the clown won't be able to come after you because daddy will chase them away, okay?" I patted Trevor on the head as he started to doze off.

Olivia stroked Trevor's hair while smiling lovingly at him before looking at me. "He's an amazing child."

"He gets the amazing genes from me." I smirked as Trevor snuggled closer to Olivia. Olivia rolled her eyes and laced our fingers together.

"I love you, Drake."

I smiled tenderly at her. "I love you too so much. You're the best thing that has ever happened to me."

Tears pooled in her green eyes, and she smiled. "You're the best thing that has ever happened to me too." She leaned over to give me a peck on the mouth. She laid her head on my chest with Trevor between us and slept.

I couldn't help but think that if I had never met Olivia, my life would be very different from how it is today.

I would most probably be still fucking any girl that caught my eye, drinking, maybe drugs, and then, prison.

And for that, I loved Olivia for saving me before my life could spiral out of control. I also loved her for giving me my son and daughter, and mostly, I loved Olivia for just simply accepting me as I was and loving me in return. I loved Olivia more than she could ever know, *heck*, I didn't even know how to describe what I felt for her with words.

As I looked down at Olivia and Trevor sleeping, my heart swelled, and I pressed a kiss to each of their heads and whispering a soft 'I love you' in their ears before laying my head on the pillow. Soon, the rhythm of Trevor and Olivia's breathing lulled me to sleep.

The End

Can't get enough of Olivia and Drake?
Make sure you sign up for the author's blog
to find out more about them!

Get these two bonus chapters and
more freebies when you sign up at
cheryl-fm.awesomeauthors.org!

Here is a sample from another story you may enjoy:

THE
ASSISTANT

Elle Brace

He was tall.

At about six-one, he towered over my five-four height and made me feel shorter than I usually did.

I watched as yet another female walked out of his office, looking flustered and flushed with embarrassment as she readjusted her business skirt.

"Ms. Johnson?" An old lady wearing a pink plaid jacket called out, pushing her glasses back up the bridge of her nose as she scanned the waiting area.

I stood up at the sound of my name and greeted her with a nervous nod and a smile that probably turned out more like a grimace.

"This way please," the lady said, escorting me into the office that nine other girls had previously entered – and exited - before me.

I clutched tightly at the folder containing my carefully listed skills and qualifications. I had worked all week to perfect it, just for a chance at this job.

"Thank you," I muttered. She gave me a reassuring pat on the shoulder before exiting the room quietly and shutting the door behind her with a soft 'thud.'

I let out a nervous sigh before turning around to meet the man I'd only ever seen on billboards, the internet and magazines. It was the first time I would see him in person.

"Name," he stated, a deep British accent lacing the singular, blunt word.

I cleared my throat and wiped my sweaty palms on my grey pencil skirt. "Hello," I said, "My name is Emily Johnson." I smiled nervously at the authority figure seated on a large leather chair behind a dark, polished marble desk so large it almost took up the entire length of the office.

He didn't glance in my direction as I walked forward and placed my resume on his desk with shaky hands.

"Take a seat," he muttered, still staring intently at his computer screen.

I nodded, even though I knew he wasn't going to be paying attention to the gesture. "Thank you." I took a seat in one of the navy coloured leather chairs that were placed in front of his desk, and gripped the arm of the chair with such force that I watched my knuckles turn white.

A few silent moments passed before his hazel green eyes flickered in my direction briefly, and then did a double take.

I felt my eyes widen slightly and I visibly swallowed from nervousness. Was I not wearing the correct clothing? Did he recognise me from somewhere? The nerves creating the knot in my stomach became stronger, and I felt the knot begin to expand.

"Ms. Johnson, was it?" he asked, raising an eyebrow as his gaze slowly scanned my attire before coming back to meet my eyes.

I gulped and nodded, causing him to smirk and get out of his seat.

"I- I have a resume…" My voice trailed off, the thought continued only by the finger I pointed toward the folder I had so painstakingly spent hours on. He wasn't paying attention to that. Instead, he walked over to where I was sitting until he stood directly in front of me.

"Get up." His tone was commanding, and I felt my body jerk out of the seat before my brain could process what was happening.

Looking at him in closer now, I saw that the magazines and pictures I had seen him in did *not* do him justice.

Who was *he*, exactly? He was Adrian Kingston, the 25-year-old-billionare-playboy who owns Kingston Corp. His father spent 23 years building the company, which now includes over 350 hotels and offices in New York City alone. I knew this because I had done my research before arriving for this job interview – to become his assistant in the Head Office of the Cooperation.

He suddenly moved closer, so close, that I could smell the mixture of cologne and aftershave he was wearing and was able to identify dimple marks in his cheeks while he smirked down at me. From this distance, it was also hard to miss the thick lashes that surrounded his eyes.

"What do you think of me, Ms. Johnson?" he asked, snaking an arm around my waist and pulling me toward his solid torso.

My eyes widened in shock and I felt my cheeks begin to turn scarlet. "I-," I stuttered, "I don't really know you well enough to answer that, s-sir." I inched my face back to put some distance between our proximity.

Adrian ignored my attempt to move away and leaned in so that his lips were near my ear. "Do I make you feel nervous?" he whispered, nibbling at my earlobe as I felt my throat go dry.

"I wouldn't say you; t- the job is what I'm nervous about. If you would look at my resume-"

His lips moved down so that he was trailing light kisses onto my collarbone. "If I don't make you nervous, do I turn you on?" he asked in a hoarse voice, pressing our bodies closer to each other than before.

"I-" I cleared my throat and frowned slightly, "I don't think what you're asking is in context as to what this interview is about. My resume-"

"Why look at a piece of paper when I have a beautiful woman standing right here?" he smirked. "You have a nice ass, by the way." I felt one of his hands slowly slide down from my waist to my rear and give it a rough squeeze.

I gasped and jumped in his hold, before pulling away in frustration. "Excuse me, Mr. Kingston. I am here solely to achieve my goal of getting this job. I don't know what *you're* trying to do – and quite frankly, I don't like it either. You're rude and disrespectful. Now, if you don't want to look over my credentials and qualifications"–I snatched the

resume that I had spent hours putting together off his desk—
"then my business here is done. Thank you for your time."

I glared and turned to leave but then remembered
something else I wanted to say. I stopped in my tracks and
turned back to face him. "Oh, and you want to know what I
think of you now? I think you're a spoiled little rich sleaze
who thinks he can have everyone he encounters, eating out
of the palm of his hand."

I slung my bag over my shoulder and stormed out of
the office without glancing back.

*So that's why all the girls that got interviewed walked out
flustered,* I thought to myself as I walked past the remaining
applicants. Good luck to them. Seriously.

"Uh, excuse me! Ms. Johnson!" The old lady who
had escorted me into Mr. Kingston's office shouted just as I
reached the halfway point down the hall.

"Yes?" I replied, looking back in confusion. Had I
forgotten something? I mentally scanned my bag.
Everything was there...

"Mr. Kingston wanted me to inform you that you
have gotten the job. You start as of right now, and your first
task is to get rid of all the remaining applicants. Welcome to
the team." She gave me a sympathetic smile before shuffling
back down the hall way and disappearing into a room on her
right.

I stood in shock for a few moments, processing the
news the lady had just revealed. I got the job? *Me?* The one
who snapped at him and called him a spoiled little rich boy?
How does that even work?

Unsure about what just happened and how I felt about it all, I decided to shake off my shock and try to complete the first task given me by the unpredictable man who was apparently my new boss. Get rid of the rest of the applicants. I scoffed internally. *Of course he'd make his newly hired assistant do his dirty work.*

I walked back to the group of girls who were giggling amongst themselves. They stopped abruptly when they noticed me smiling nervously in their direction.

"I thought you were already rejected by him," a red head sneered. "Back for more? Talk about desperate." The others laughed.

I tried to keep the urge to glare buried deep within me. My nerves have now been replaced by anger. "Actually, I was just told that I was hired," I told them with a sarcastic smile. "My first job is to get rid of you lot. Maybe you can come back later for more? Oh wait – the job is already taken. Sorry. Have a good day."

"Yeah right," the red head scoffed. "We saw how you left his office. He didn't hire you. You're just trying to get rid of the competition because you're too intimidated by us." She rolled her eyes and settled in her seat smugly, looking at the other girls.

I sighed and rubbed my temple. "Yes. I'm so intimidated by you all. How will I ever survive knowing you're all out there, being the perfect little bitches you're all being right now?" I pretended to fake sob, before my face turned blank again. "Now, on behalf of Mr. Kingston, please leave, or I will call security to escort you lovely ladies out."

I didn't even know if the building had security, let alone the number to call.

The 5 pairs of eyes glared up at me, and I felt as if I was shrinking under their gaze. The red head spoke again. "You're pathetic. We're all smart enough to know that you're lying. Adrian wouldn't hire someone like *you*. You're too short and *way* too curvy. He'd want someone slim and petite, not to mention someone who actually has a pretty face." Her gaze focused on the thick black rims that surrounded the lenses that helped me read clearer, and I felt my temper slowly taking over the rational side of me. I was about to burst when a deep voice kept it from happening.

"Ladies."

Adrian's voice came from behind me. I caught the smell of his cologne before I felt two large hands being placed on my shoulders.

"What Ms. Johnson is saying is correct," he told them. "She has officially been hired by me. Thank you for coming in today, but you are not needed anymore. Leave, or I *will* call security to drag you out."

The 5 girls were frozen with shock, but the red haired girl recovered quickly. "But Adrian, surely we're more qualified-"

"I have personally looked over Ms. Johnson's qualifications and found her to be the perfect candidate. This discussion is over. Have a nice day." He dismissed them coolly, before I felt his warm breath on my neck.

"Come into my office once they leave so I can brief you on your role as my assistant."

I nodded stiffly, conscious of the proximity between our bodies.

"Don't worry, I won't try anything." He chuckled softly. "Even though I want to."

He pulled away and I turned to catch his smirk just before it slipped off his face and he turned to leave.

I turned back to the girls – who were looking at me as if they were measuring what coffin would fit me best – and gave them a small smile. "Thank you for your time," I repeated, stepping aside as an indication for them to leave.

"This isn't over, you obese pig," the red head sneered before shoving her handbag up her slender arm and stomping past me. "I'll get you fired within the next month. This job is *mine*." The other girls followed after her.

I looked down at my body and sighed. Yes, I was pretty large in the chest and rear area, but I was pretty slim everywhere else. I went for regular jogs in a park nearby and ate clean once a week. I shook my self-esteem issues out of my mind temporarily, and entered Adrian's office after a heavy sigh.

"I'm going to be very quick with this because I have a meeting in 10 minutes," he said, even before I closed the door. "You are to learn my daily schedule by heart. From the time I open my eyes in bed 'till the time I shut them. You are to know what coffee I drink and have it at my desk by 8:55AM every day. I only like it made by a certain barista at a specific Starbucks four blocks from here. You are to know what size I am in everything – including underwear – and keep a spare item of clothing on you at all times in case something goes wrong. You only get a half hour lunch break but will get a full hour on Saturdays." As he spoke he was shuffling though a stack of papers on his desk. When he finished, he handed them all to me.

"You are also responsible for any irrelevant paperwork that comes through to me. This," he pointed at the paper on top of the pile, "is my planner. You are responsible for organising it fortnightly and bringing it to my apartment every Sunday evening. You can email it to me as well but I prefer to have the original copy in case I decide to make any adjustments. Your working hours are 8:30AM until 6:00PM, but there will be *a lot* of evenings where you and I will stay back late in the office to manage larger projects. Mrs. Brown, the lady who escorted you here, will show you where your new desk is located. You answer your phone at all times and only refer the important ones back to me. Mrs. Brown will give you a list of who to let through. The line for my office is the number one on speed dial on your phone. Any questions?"

I stared at him blankly before I felt my eyelids blink. "Yes, how do I know what paperwork is irr-"

"Mrs. Brown will explain what is and what is not important for me to see or do, and that will become *your* responsibility. Now, if you're not planning on wasting my time with any more of your imprudent questions, I'm going to leave now."

I frowned and opened my mouth to defend myself but remembered he was my new boss so I just nodded and began to turn around to leave the office.

"Oh, and Ms. Johnson?" he called out, making me turn back. "I suggest you keep a spare pair of underwear in your drawer at all times as well. I'm pretty sure you're going to be needing them." He smirked before dismissing me once again, leaving me confused with his statement.

Why on Earth will I be needing a spare pair of underwear at work? I thought to myself as I walked over to the room I had seen Mrs. Brown enter previously. "Um, excuse me, Mrs. Brown...?" I knocked on the open door gently.

The woman looked up from the papers in front of her and pulled her glasses back up the bridge of her nose before smiling. "Ah yes, Emily dear. Call me Suzie. Mr. Kingston has briefed you on your job as his assistant, I take it? You're looking rather confused. Take a seat, I'll explain it to you in more detail then show you to your new office shortly. Aren't you excited? This is an excellent job! And great pay, if I do say so myself!" She grinned brightly, and I felt my lips tug into a smile as well.

I mentally agreed with her. It was a great job, I just mentally prayed that I was going to be able to stay sane around the most attractive male in America (literally, he was voted the number one 'hottie' in *Cosmopolitan*).

***

"DID YOU GET THE JOB? IS HE REALLY AS HOT AS EVERYONE SAYS HE IS? DID HE MAKE

YOUR HEART MELT WITH HIS CHARM? DID YOU HAVE SEX?"

My best friend's overly excited voice screeched from my iPhone's speaker.

My eyes widened at the last question and I felt my cheeks getting warmer. Even though she couldn't see me, I knew Amy was trying to make me squirm. "You're so blushing right now. I can feel it in my blood! You had sex, didn't you?! Was he amazing? Ask him to do me!" I heard her sigh and I almost gagged into the speaker.

"Amy!"

"What?" she said innocently.

"We did *not* have sex. It was a formal meeting. He's pretty rude. And throws a lot of... suggestive comments, but yes, I got the job!" I squealed, grinning at the blank television screen in my apartment.

More squealing erupted from the speaker of my iPhone and I felt my hand automatically move the phone away in order to keep my hearing intact. Once she was done, I placed the phone back on my ear. "Thank you." I laughed as I heard her catch her breath.

"We have to celebrate tonight! I'll call Molly and Claire! We'll go down to-" Her voice got cut off by a soft beep and I frowned and looked at my phone. An unsaved number blinked in my face, signaling that there was someone on the other line. "Sorry, Amy, there's someone else on the line and I don't have their number saved. We'll definitely go out to celebrate! Text me the details, okay?

Bye!" I quickly hung up and pressed the green button to answer the other call. "Hello?"

"Ms. Johnson, I need you to come to the office immediately." It was unmistakably Adrian Kingston's deep, British voice. My eyes widened in shock. "There is some paperwork here that we need to sort through together and it needs to be sent in by *tonight*. I expect you'll be here in less than half an hour?"

"Sir, I live a good 20 minutes away from the office. It'll take me a little longer than half an hour to get there." I stuttered nervously. A night call *already?* I still didn't even know the location to my office properly!

"If you stopped complaining over the phone and got moving, it wouldn't take long at all," he snapped. "I'll see you in half an hour." The line went dead. I detached the phone from my ear and stared uncomprehendingly at the blank screen, before shaking out of my daze and rushing back to my bedroom to get dressed for work.

I called Amy as I pulled out my white business shirt and black pencil skirt and thrashed my pajama bottoms off. Amy answered on the first ring. "Hey! I just confirmed with the girls, they're up for it!" she said excitedly.

I groaned as I stubbed my toe on the corner of my bed before zipping up my pencil skirt and tucking the shirt in neatly. "Ames, I'm so sorry. He's already called me in to fill out some paperwork that needed to be mailed by tonight, apparently. I'm so sorry, raincheck?" I asked as I pulled my semi-dry hair into a sleek pony tail and applying a coat of light pink lipstick. Thank god I had natural ringlets that didn't frizz after every shower I had.

"Already? Damn, girl, you're going to have your work cut out for you! Don't apologise, it was your celebration drink, you banana!" She laughed, before gasping. "You better be wearing sexy lingerie! Late nights alone in the office with a sex god? I think I can predict what's going to happen." I could practically feel Amy wink as I rolled my eyes and put my black pumps on and grabbed the bag I prepared once I got home.

"Amy, get your mind out of the gutter," I joked. "Anyway, I have to go. He expects me to be there in less than half an hour. I'm so sorry for cancelling on you, girls. I'll make it up to you guys, I promise!"

Amy scoffed. "Shut up! You're putting the blame on yourself as if you don't have a good enough reason to be cancelling! Say hi to the sexy beast for me, will you? I'll let you go now because you've just wasted 5 minutes talking to me."

"I'm a woman. Multi-tasking is in our blood," I laughed. "I'm leaving my apartment now. Love you!"

We both disconnected the phone and I made my way to call the nearest cab.

This is how it all began.

If you enjoyed this sample then look for The Assistant on Amazon!

Other books you might enjoy:

Marriage by Law
N.K. Pockett
Available on Amazon!

Acknowledgements

Thank you to my agent Le-an! Thanks so much for making this little hobby of mine into a reality by spotting the book on Wattpad! Also, thank you for being so patient with my never-ending questions and late replies over email! (Sorry about that!) Also, thanks to my editor AJ for helping me pick and look through all the silly mistakes my younger self has made when writing this! Also, thanks to the people at Blvnp Incorporated for this exciting and brilliant opportunity!

Special thanks to Rush Mendon for the amazing and gorgeous cover! You are absolutely brilliant! I would also like to thank all you lovely readers on Wattpad because if it weren't for all of your support, this book wouldn't be where it is today! I do love you all oh so much! You guys deserve a special shout out and here it is!

About the Author

Cheryl F. M. is a writer in her spare time who began writing on Wattpad, a platform where people share and read stories online. A huge Potterhead, she spends most of her free time re-watching the Harry Potter movies. She is currently studying in the field of Business Management and loves reading books with genres such as action, comedy, fantasy and romance.